"What?" Mollie's shocked voice rang with a note of panic.

Jago eyeballed her, a grimly determined set to his mouth. "I want you to come with me to her party this weekend. As my fiancée."

Mollie looked as if he had asked her to fly to the moon and back and pick up a souvenir satellite on the way. Her mouth opened and closed, her hands tightened around her glass and then she placed it down on the table beside her, the surface of the water shivering slightly. "There's no way I can do that, Jago. It's unfair of you to ask me to."

"I'm not asking you. I'm telling you."

Wilde Billionaire Brothers

Brothers Jago, Jack and Jonas were born into the Wilde family's billion-dollar world. But just as quickly as their privileged lives started, their parents' lives tragically ended. So, they began to build their barriers to love as high as the skyscrapers that they owned. But can three exceptional women convince Jago, Jack and Jonas to replace reason with irrational—but oh-so irresistible!—desire...?

Take a walk on the Wilde side with...

Jago and Mollie's story

Available now!

Jack and Sylvie's story

Jonas and Tessa's story

Coming soon!

FAKE ENGAGEMENT ARRANGEMENT

MELANIE MILBURNE

PRESENTS

If you purchased this book without a cover you should be aware that this book is stolen property. It was reported as "unsold and destroyed" to the publisher, and neither the author nor the publisher has received any payment for this "stripped book."

ISBN-13: 978-1-335-21316-7

Fake Engagement Arrangement

Copyright © 2025 by Melanie Milburne

Recycling programs for this product may not exist in your area.

All rights reserved. No part of this book may be used or reproduced in any manner whatsoever without written permission.

Without limiting the author's and publisher's exclusive rights, any unauthorized use of this publication to train generative artificial intelligence (AI) technologies is expressly prohibited.

This is a work of fiction. Names, characters, places and incidents are either the product of the author's imagination or are used fictitiously. Any resemblance to actual persons, living or dead, businesses, companies, events or locales is entirely coincidental.

For questions and comments about the quality of this book, please contact us at CustomerService@Harlequin.com.

TM and ® are trademarks of Harlequin Enterprises ULC.

 Harlequin Enterprises ULC
22 Adelaide St. West, 41st Floor
Toronto, Ontario M5H 4E3, Canada
www.Harlequin.com

Printed in Lithuania

Melanie Milburne read her first Harlequin novel at the age of seventeen in between studying for her final exams. After completing a master's degree in education, she decided to write a novel, and thus her career as a romance author was born. Melanie is an ambassador for the Australian Childhood Foundation and a keen dog lover and trainer. She enjoys long walks in the Tasmanian bush. In 2015 Melanie won the HOLT Medallion, a prestigious award honoring outstanding literary talent.

Books by Melanie Milburne

Harlequin Presents

The Billion-Dollar Bride Hunt
One Night in My Rival's Bed
Illicit Italian Nights

The Scandalous Campbell Sisters

Shy Innocent in the Spotlight
A Contract for His Runaway Bride

Weddings Worth Billions

Cinderella's Invitation to Greece
Nine Months After That Night
Forbidden Until Their Snowbound Night

Visit the Author Profile page
at Harlequin.com for more titles.

In loving memory of my dearest and oldest friend, Ina Shepherd. We became firm friends from the first time I arrived in Tasmania as a lonely young mom starting from scratch all over again when my husband moved around the globe for his surgical career. I was so blessed to have known you and loved and been loved by you for so long.
Rest in peace. xxxx

CHAPTER ONE

MOLLIE WAS AT the reception desk at the beauty clinic, looking at the latest cancellation on the computer diary. This was the third cancellation this week, and it was only Wednesday. And all of them were her clients. The economy was suffering, and as a result so was she. But wasn't that the story of her life.

It could have been so different if you had married Jago Wilde...

The thought drifted into her head, and she quickly shoved it away, like slamming a door on an unwelcome guest. Too many times that wayward thought would catch her off guard, torturing her with what could have been. Two years had passed, and still, every day she thought of Jago. Every day and every night. She still found herself reaching for him in her bed. No one had taken his place and she wondered if anyone ever would. She was trying to break herself of the habit of thinking of him, but her dire financial circumstances kept reminding her of what she could have had if she hadn't jilted him. Money. Security.

Safety. A sense of connection she had never felt in her life before him.

The salon door opened, and Mollie looked up from the computer with a welcoming smile, hoping it was a walk-in client to fill her empty hour, only for her smile to freeze on her face like a wax model. Her blood chilled to ice in her veins, her hands trembled, her heart thumped, and her breath halted.

It couldn't be him. It couldn't be real. She must be hallucinating. Was it really Jago Wilde standing there? Was it a trick of her brain, an apparition brought on by the stress she was under with her worries over her younger brother? She opened and closed her mouth but couldn't get her voice to work. It was rare for her to be lost for words. Rare for her not to be able to stand up for herself, but the circumstances surrounding her break-up with Jago brought hot shame ripening on her cheeks like blood red apples. How could she face him without triggering the feelings she had tried to smother with work and responsibilities? How could she see him without breaking her agreement with his powerful grandfather?

Jago gave a cynical twist of his mouth that passed for a smile, his dark blue eyes scanning her like a laser beam. 'Got a minute for a chat?' His deep, mellifluous voice stroked down her spine like the caress of his warm, broad-spanned hand. Oh, how she had missed his voice. That gorgeous baritone with its crisp English accent that spoke of wealth and privilege from the cradle. The way his voice matched his appearance and yet *tall, dark and handsome* was an understatement. His movie star good looks were beyond traffic-stopping: he could stop a meteor mid-descent. The way he carried himself with confidence, assurance of his place in the world, and yes, even a generous dose of the legendary Wilde arrogance was etched in the landscape of his features. The jet-black hair, the slash of prominent eyebrows, the deep-set, intelligent eyes that could melt stone. The sculptured lips that could break into an easy smile that could make a marble statue's legs tremble, let alone Mollie's.

But Jago wasn't smiling at her now. The cynical slant on his mouth didn't reach his eyes, and it made her stomach clench like a fist.

Mollie was relieved her boss wasn't in that day because Shelagh discouraged personal visits at the clinic. Mollie's job was already hanging by a gossamer thread because of all the days she had taken off to rescue her brother Eliot from yet another disaster. She couldn't lose her job over Jago Wilde—that would be the ultimate humiliation.

'I have back-to-back clients,' Mollie said, holding his gaze with an effort. 'I'm expecting my next one any minute now.' Turns out she was a stellar liar. Years of being shunted from foster home to foster home had honed her skills in mendacity to the point where sometimes she even convinced herself she was telling the truth. Like that she no longer loved Jago Wilde. She didn't miss him or want him any more. That she didn't regret signing that wretched agreement written by his autocratic grandfather, Maxwell Wilde, who had been keen to get her out of his grandson's life before she soiled it and the Wilde name with her trailer trash background. If she hadn't thought there was truth in what Maxwell believed, that she would indeed taint the man she had loved, she would have fought and fought hard. She wasn't a quitter, hence the years of chasing after her brother, searching for him in dark, shadowy, murderous alleyways, paying off his drug debts to keep him out of prison or worse. Holding the basin while he was hideously ill after an all-night bender. Doing all she could to make up for what she had failed to do when they were children.

Jago's eyes penetrated hers like a powerful searchlight, an inscrutable glint showing in his. 'Have a drink with me after work.'

It was typical that Jago commanded rather than asked, and it was also typical Mollie was tempted to obey his command. Just to see what he had to say. Just to spend a few minutes in his company to prove to herself she was finally over him. That she could be in his presence for half an hour and not want him feverishly. He was standing on the other side of the reception counter, close enough for her to see the midnight blue of his eyes and the ink-black lashes that framed them. His eyes had always fascinated, captivated and entranced her. They were an unusual navy shade reminding her of a deep ocean with unknowable depths. She could pick up the exotic spice and woodsy notes of his aftershave, and she had to stop her nostrils from flaring to take in more of his addictive smell. Her eyes moved from his to glance at his mouth. Big mistake. His mouth was her kryptonite. One kiss from his lips when they first met had made her stomach somersault and her pulse race out of control. She had never been able to resist those tantalising and skilful lips. She had felt them on every inch of her body, and being in his presence again triggered a storm of need in her flesh, and she had a feeling he knew it. His mouth was sensually contoured with evenly full lips and a well-defined philtrum ridge like he had been designed by a master sculptor. He hadn't shaved in a couple of days, and she suppressed a shiver as she remembered how those sexy bristles felt against her soft skin.

But his face had changed since they had parted. He now had a deep line carved between his prominent brows as if he had spent a lot of time frowning over the last two years. And his thick black hair was longer than it used to be and brushed back from his face in a careless manner, as if he had run his fingers through it recently.

Mollie gripped the counter that divided them in an effort to control her hands from reaching out to touch him, to see if the electric energy was still there when they touched skin-on-skin. But she could feel it anyway—the tightening of the atmosphere as if all the oxygen particles had shifted. A galaxy of dust motes of desire circling between them. A palpable current in the air that made it almost impossible for her to hide the affect he was having on her.

But hide it she did.

Mollie gave him an arch look. 'A drink? Is that all you want, Jago?'

His eyes darkened to pools of blue ink, glinting, measuring, unwavering. 'I have a proposal for you.'

Her brows rose in a haughty manner. 'Not another one?'

A dark gleam shone in his eyes as they held hers. 'This one you would be a fool not to accept.' There was a hard edge to his voice that hinted at the bitterness that still simmered in his veins. Bitterness her actions had caused.

In spite of her misgivings about spending any more time in his company, Mollie was tempted to hear him out. What sort of proposal did he have in mind? And what would happen if his elderly grandfather found out they had met up again? The agreement she had signed with Maxwell Wilde had forbidden her from ever contacting Jago and from ever explaining to him why she had jilted him the day before their wedding. Forbidden her from speaking to the press for a tell-all interview. Forbidden her to tell Jago about the AI-generated sextortion she was a victim of and how Jago's grandfather had presented her with an ultimatum to make it all go away. Maxwell could make the AI images of her disappear, but she had to disappear too. She had been paid handsomely to go away, and go away she had—all the way to Scotland. She would have gone farther if not for her brother. But of course, the money had eventually run out due to her brother's chronic addiction and mental health issues, and she was starting to wonder if any amount of money would save him from the same self-destruction of their mother. But Eliot was her only living relative, and she would do anything and everything in her power to save him. He was currently on another long stint in a rehab centre, and it had drained every penny from her bank account to keep him there. She couldn't remember the last time she had eaten a proper meal. Beans on toast or instant noodles had been her only source of nutrition and would be until her next pay cheque…if her boss didn't let her go due to the downturn in business.

'How did you find me?' Mollie asked in a cool tone that belied the tumult of her emotions.

'I've always known where you were.'

Mollie tried not to show her stunned reaction, but even so her eyes widened in shock. He had known for two years that she was living and working in the suburbs of Edinburgh? She moistened her talcum powder–dry lips and schooled her features back into some semblance of neutrality. She couldn't imagine Maxwell Wilde would have told him, but who else knew? No one. 'Who told you?'

Something passed across Jago's face like a faint ripple across a calm body of water. But his jaw tightened as if he was biting down on his molars. His diamond-hard look drilled into her gaze. 'It wasn't my grandfather. The only thing he told me was what a lucky escape I had when you jilted me.'

Mollie disguised a swallow and let go of the counter, opening and closing her stiff fingers. She kept her expression impassive, but her stomach was churning enough to make butter for every supplier of shortbread in the country. Possibly even the world.

'And no doubt you agree with him?'

'There are some things my grandfather and I do not see eye to eye on,' Jago said with an unreadable look. 'What time do you finish work?'

'I don't think it's a good idea if we—'

'Meet me at my hotel at six this evening. I'll be waiting in the bar.'

He slipped his hand inside his jacket pocket and took out a business card and, taking a pen from the counter, scrawled the address of his hotel on the back and then handed it to her. She looked at it like it was a hand grenade that could blow up in her face. But then again, it could. A meeting with her ex-fiancé, in public, was flirting with danger.

Terrifying, but tempting danger.

Jago sat slowly sipping a single malt whisky and kept his eyes trained on the entrance to the stylish bar of his Edinburgh hotel. He was taking a gamble Mollie would show up, but he was determined to talk to her in private. A hotel bar was hardly private, but if he could get her to agree to take their discussion to his suite, then even better. Seeing her again had triggered things in him he didn't want triggered: anger, bitterness, humiliation at what she had done. And yes, those other feelings he didn't want to think too deeply about. The feelings Mollie had stirred in him from the moment he met her. The connection with her had been instant and intense, reminding him of how his father must have felt about his mother and vice versa. Was it love? He had never acknowledged it, but he had a worrying sense it could well have been something close to it. But Mollie's jilting of him had blown it out like a flickering match stick in a stiff breeze. The flame was gone, but the match head was still warm. He had to make sure it wasn't in any danger of being reignited. He would have kept his distance, like he had doggedly done for the last two years, mostly out of stubborn pride. But since his grandmother's recent fall, which the doctors were worried she might not fully recover from, he needed Mollie's help, and he was prepared to pay for it. Besides, she had accepted money before, so he was confident she would accept it again, especially the eye-watering amount he was offering.

Jago leaned forward and put his whisky glass down on the table in front of him, his eyes catching sight of a brunette head outside the hotel. His pulse leapt, his blood throbbed, and his anger and bitterness boiled. Mollie was no longer dressed in her white beauty-clinic uniform with its grey trim but in a simple long-sleeved black dress that clung to her slim body in all the right places. Places he had caressed with his lips and tongue and hands. A shiver went down his spine like a streak of lightning, and he drew in a harsh breath to remind himself to keep on task. This was not the time to think of the red-hot lust that brought them together from day one in a cataclysmic storm. It was not the time to recall how his body had possessed the tight, wet, silky warmth of hers until he lost all conscious thought. She had been his most exciting lover, and no one had ever come close to measuring up to her. Which only made him all the more furious and intent on drawing a final line under their relationship once his grandmother's health situation was sorted one way or the other.

Jago stood as she approached and waved his hand to a deep velvet chair close to his. 'Take a seat. What would you like to drink?'

'Water is fine, thank you.' Mollie sat and elegantly crossed her slim legs, her hands clasping her evening purse with tense fingers. But as if she sensed his glance at her hands, she loosened her hold on the purse and then released a long, steadying breath like someone about to start a yoga session after a stressful day. Even though her expression was as blank as an unpainted canvas, there was a flicker of tension in her eyes. A barely perceptible movement like a stagehand covertly shifting the set pieces around out of sight of the audience.

Jago waited until the waiter had served Mollie a tall glass of ice-water and moved away again before he spoke. 'Busy day at the clinic?' He raised his own glass to his lips and kept his eyes on hers as he took a sip.

'Busy enough.' Her mouth tightened and her gaze shifted, focusing on the open neck of his business shirt. He saw her throat move up and down, a telltale sign of nervousness she was clearly at great pains to hide. She glanced around the bar then turned back to face him, another flicker of worry passing through her gaze.

'Relax, Mollie,' Jago said, leaning back in his seat and putting his glass down beside him. 'There are no paps around to document this auspicious moment.'

A frown tugged at her brow, and she shifted in her seat as if there were marbles beneath her. Then she tossed the mane of her light brown hair over her shoulders, her expression masked. 'What did you want to speak to me about? You mentioned a proposal. I'm guessing it's not a marriage one like the last time.' Her tone was cool with a hint of mockery that ignited his anger all over again. And that was what he wanted ignited—anger, not those other feelings.

'My grandmother is unwell.' He kept his gaze locked on her so he could gauge her reaction.

Mollie blinked and swept her tongue over her lips, her eyes showing compassion rather than the cool indifference he was expecting. 'I'm sorry to hear that. Is she in hospital?'

'She has been but is now at Wildewood Manor. She had a fall and has broken her arm and suffered a concussion.'

'I'm sorry. It must be so difficult for her.'

'That's not the worst of it.' Jago kept his gaze trained on hers. 'Gran has some memory issues as a result of the fall.' He waited a beat and continued. 'She thinks we are still engaged to be married.'

Mollie's eyes widened for a fraction of a second before she adopted a bland expression once more. 'That must be quite inconvenient for you having to explain that we are no longer—'

'I have chosen not to explain that to her.'

Mollie stiffened like a ventriloquist's puppet suddenly jerked upright. 'What?' Her shocked voice rang with a note of panic.

Jago eyeballed her, a grimly determined set to his mouth. 'I want you to come with me to her eighty-fifth birthday party this weekend. As my fiancée.'

Mollie looked as if he had asked her to fly to the moon and back and pick up a souvenir satellite on the way. Her mouth opened and closed, her hands tightened around her glass, and then she placed it down on the table beside her, the surface of the water shivering slightly. 'There's no way I can do that, Jago. It's unfair of you to ask me to.'

'I'm not asking you. I'm telling you.'

Her grey-blue eyes challenged his, and his blood pulsed and leapt in excitement. He had always found her strong-willed spirit a turn-on. It was one of the things he had missed about her since she'd walked out on him—the fiery spats that always ended up in bed. The sun never went down on their anger; he made sure of it. The combustion of their lust for each other had been cataclysmic, and even though he did everything in his power to erase those sensational sensual sessions from his mind, nothing worked. Mollie was branded on his body, his brain, in his blood. He could feel it now: the heat, the throb, the tightening of his flesh. The hunger. The raw raging need nothing would satisfy but her.

'What does your grandfather think of this…plan of yours?' she asked with a cautious look cast in his direction without fully meeting his gaze.

'I haven't told him yet. I thought I'd surprise him.'

The colour leached from her face like a cartoon character, and her gaze snapped back to his. 'I seem to recall your grandfather isn't one for surprises.'

'People can change.'

She gave a snort and reached for her water with a not-quite-steady hand. 'I haven't yet seen a leopard prowling around without its spots.' The bitterness in her tone didn't surprise Jago. His grandfather wasn't known for his charm, but he was legendary at cutting insults and masterful manipulation. Jago and his brothers had been on the receiving end of Maxwell Wilde's vicious tongue too many times to count. But since his grandfather's stroke a year ago, the old man was not as powerful as he liked to think he was. And Jago was going to use it to his advantage. The press so far had not been privy to how much less powerful Maxwell currently was, and Jago was making the most of it.

Jago leaned back in his chair, one ankle crossing over his knee in a casual fashion, his finger idly flicking the toggle on the zipper of his Italian leather ankle boot. 'Of course it goes without saying I'll pay you for your time.'

Twin spots of colour came flooding back into her cheeks, and her mouth flattened. 'How much?'

'Double what my grandfather paid you.'

Mollie gaped at him, her eyes as wide as a cornered animal. 'He told you about that?' Her voice came out as a shocked thread of sound that was barely audible.

Jago slanted his lips in a cynical smile. 'Don't act so surprised, my love. I made it my business to find out what price had induced you to make a fool of me.'

Mollie looked down at her hands in her lap, her fingers gripping her purse like it was a lifeline. 'Please don't say that. We both know you didn't love me.' Her voice was strained and her colour high.

'There are much worse things I could say, so you should be thankful I chose that.'

Jago was still confused about his feelings for her, back then and now. So many emotions had thundered through him when she'd jilted him. Shock, humiliation, anger, rage, despair, a deep, burning sense of betrayal—the list was endless. How could he have been so easily hoodwinked by her? She was a consummate actor, able to play the role of devoted fiancée for four months while all the time waiting for her chance to grab the money and run. As sums of money went, especially given his family's wealth, it hadn't been that huge an amount. But clearly it had been enough for her to make a new life for herself, without him. It infuriated Jago he had genuinely believed she had fallen in love with him. He wasn't the sort of guy to be easily deceived, and yet she had done it and done it convincingly. He knew Hollywood actors who couldn't have done a better job of fooling him. He knew he should direct most of his anger at his grandfather for paying her such a sum, but he couldn't find it in himself to forgive Mollie for taking it. Why had she done it? If she had needed money, he would have gladly given it to her. He still had trouble accepting she was a gold-digger, but all the evidence pointed to it. What other interpretation could he have? She chose to humiliate him by pretending to be madly in love with him for months on end, sharing his bed, wearing his specially designed engagement ring, looking up at him adoringly. How had he not seen through it? Jago used to pride himself on being able to spot a gold-digger from afar, but in Mollie's case he had got it so wrong. She had made a fool out of him in front of the world, and that he would *never* forgive.

But now, all Jago felt was a need to protect his grandmother, and if he had to bribe Mollie to play a little game of make-believe with him, then so be it.

CHAPTER TWO

MOLLIE WAS TRYING to control her reaction to Jago's outrageous offer. He was willing to pay her a jaw dropping amount of money to pretend she was still his fiancée for his grandmother's sake. How could she accept? She mentally pictured the paltry balance in her bank account. How could she *not* accept? Did she even have a choice? It didn't appear so by the steely light of determination in Jago's eyes as he watched her like a hawk about to swoop down to collect its much-prized prey.

Besides, there was Eliot to consider.

There was always her brother to consider. His issues had consumed her life to the point that she wondered if she would ever be free of the burden of worry she carried around like a backpack of boulders. Eliot needed long-term rehabilitation and therapy, but those things did not come cheaply. She had already spent every penny Maxwell Wilde had given her on getting help for her brother. Help that had failed time and time again, because no sooner would Eliot be clean for a day or even a week or two, his demons from the past would come back to haunt him like cruel, taunting ghosts.

Mollie let go of her purse and picked up her waterglass for something to do with her hands. The cold glass with its cubes of ice bobbing inside it reminded her of the ice around Jago's heart. He hated her. She could see it reflected back at her in those impossibly blue eyes. It pained her to see how much he loathed her when once he'd looked at her with eyes gleaming with passion and respect.

Who in her life had ever looked at her that way?

No one.

Mollie hadn't told him anything of her background, and she wondered now if that had been a mistake on her part. But she had spent her life trying to forget about the chaos of her childhood. She had made up a new version so she didn't have to suffer the retelling of a terrible tale of neglect and abuse and deadly violence. She hadn't even told Jago she had a younger half-brother. It was easier to edit Eliot out of her backstory so she didn't have to explain the tragic circumstances that had made Eliot such a train wreck. Circumstances she should have protected him from but had failed to do so. That was another burden she carried through life: the guilt of not protecting her younger brother from a vile predator.

Mollie took a sip of water to relieve the dryness of her mouth then put the glass back down. She straightened in her seat, forcing herself to meet Jago's gaze. 'What's your grandfather going to say when I suddenly appear by your side?' The thought of facing Maxwell Wilde was almost as daunting as seeing Jago again. Would Maxwell sue her for breach of contract? He was a powerful man with contacts and connections in the upper echelons of society.

'He won't be happy about it, but he's not the one I'm concerned about right now. Gran is my focus.'

Mollie knew Jago and his brothers Jonas and Jack had never been close to their overbearing grandfather, but they each adored their gentle grandmother, Elsie. Orphaned when young children, they had been raised by their grandparents. Jago had always been reluctant to talk about his childhood, she assumed because of the grief of losing his parents when he was only five years old, which had made it easier for her not to talk about hers. His grandmother had always been lovely towards Mollie on the handful of occasions she had seen her, and she had often thought of her in the two years that had passed. But Mollie had never warmed to Maxwell Wilde because she had met his type so many times before. A wonderful friend but a dangerous enemy. Charming on the surface but manipulative and conniving if you fell out of favour with him. Which unfortunately Mollie had by not being considered good enough for his middle grandson. Maxwell had done a background check on her and uncovered some of the dark secrets she had so desperately tried to keep hidden. Eliot's time in youth detention; her run-in with the police as a teenager when she stole a jacket from a store because she was cold and didn't have the money to buy one.

But there was one new dark mark against Mollie's name which she only found out via Maxwell Wilde the day before her wedding to Jago. While doing research on her, Maxwell had discovered an extortion plot and presented her with a solution to her dilemma. Suddenly finding herself the victim of an AI sextortion turned her world upside down and inside out. The horror and shock of seeing those explicit images of her about to be uploaded to a popular porn site had made her sick to her stomach. The panic. The dread. The drumbeat of fear that if her brother saw those ghastly images, it would send him into another downward spiral, from which he might not recover. There hadn't been time to even talk to Jago about it because he had flown to New York for a meeting and couldn't be contacted. She thought of how those sickening images might destroy his reputation as well as hers, which was why when Maxwell Wilde swooped in and assured her he could make it all go away by paying off the extortionist, she had agreed to his terms.

Those terrible, heartbreaking but totally necessary terms.

How could she face Maxwell now? Those terms had demanded she disappear from Jago's life and never return. Mollie didn't know if or what Maxwell had told Jago about her and her brother's history. She didn't know if Jago knew about the sextortion that had come close to destroying her life and, by association, perhaps his. But hadn't it already destroyed her life? Her hopes and dreams for a better life—a life where she didn't have to worry about her brother or try and scrape enough money together to help him— had been part of why she'd wanted to marry Jago. She had loved him, yes, although she had never heard him say those words back to her. It hadn't mattered to her back then. She hadn't allowed it to matter. She had only whispered those words once to him while he was sleeping. She had loved him and wanted to be his wife and pretend her old life belonged to someone else. But of course, her past came back to haunt her, and it was particularly humiliating that it was Jago's grandfather who had uncovered her secrets and lies.

'I heard your grandfather had a stroke a year ago,' Mollie said to fill the silence. 'Is he doing okay?' Mollie wasn't a vengeful person, but she couldn't help feeling there had been a bit of karma at play when she read the news report of Maxwell Wilde's stroke. He'd survived it but was now confined to a wheelchair and was working doggedly at his rehabilitation. Whether it had been a success or not hadn't thus far been reported.

Jago picked up his whisky glass and twirled the amber contents for a moment, his expression inscrutable. 'He's found the limitations thrust upon him hard to accept, and he's made my grandmother's life difficult as a result.' He put the glass down again and uncrossed his ankle, his eyes hard as they held hers. 'So will you agree to my offer?'

Mollie rolled her lips together, trying her best to resist the outrageous sum he was offering for a weekend of playing pretend. This was her chance, quite possibly her only chance, of getting Eliot the help he needed. The drugs he was hooked on had done so much damage to him, but there was a possibility that he could recover with long-term rehab and psychotherapy. What other way was open to her to raise that amount of money? Winning the lottery, but what were the chances of that? Wouldn't it be better to accept Jago's offer, for his grandmother's sake as well as Mollie's brother's?

'How long do you want me for?' As soon as Mollie uttered the words, she wished she had chosen different ones. She could feel betraying warmth stealing into her cheeks and reached for her glass of water to take a sip, lowering her gaze from the steely glint of his.

'That depends.'

She glanced at him again, her hand tightening around her drink. The cold from the glass was seeping through her skin into her body. In spite of the flickering warmth of the fireplace nearby, she shivered. 'On what?'

'My grandmother is quite unwell. The doctors aren't willing to give us any certainty on whether or not she will recover her memory. But we will start with her birthday party weekend and see how it goes from there.'

Mollie put her glass down and then began to absently rub the knuckle of her empty ring finger. She had loved the ring Jago had chosen for her and was surprised Maxwell hadn't insisted on her handing it back when he paid her to go away. She had offered it to him, but he'd shaken his head, his faded blue eyes cold. It was as if he thought the priceless ring was already tainted by her wearing it. Mollie had planned to post it back to Jago, but then remembering the terms of the non-disclosure agreement Maxwell had insisted she sign, that option was off the table. She was not to contact Jago under any circumstances. She'd held on to the ring for weeks, taking it out and looking at it as a reminder of what her engagement to Jago had represented: a chance to change her life for the better and help Eliot finally slay his demons. To believe in love conquering all. But one day when she'd opened the drawer where she kept the ring, she found it was gone. Sold by her brother to pay off a drug debt. It confirmed to Mollie the hopelessness of her dream. Happily-ever-afters didn't happen to people like her. Dreams didn't get a chance to fly. Hope could only hold out so long, no matter how driven and determined you were.

There had been an element of compromise about Mollie accepting Jago's marriage proposal after only four months of dating, but she had loved him and hoped his feelings would grow for her. He had certainly acted like a man in love. He was an attentive and considerate lover. He had patiently listened when she'd vented about a difficult client or when she'd told him of some new skin product she was excited about using. She had fooled herself—like a lot of women did—that one day he would say those magical three little words. He hadn't, and now he never would. Not after what she had done. He hated her. He loathed her. He thought her a gold-digger. And if she told him the truth, there was a chance he wouldn't believe her.

No one had ever told Mollie they loved her, not even her brother.

'What did you do with my engagement ring?' Jago asked, glancing at her left hand. 'Sell it?'

Mollie stilled her hands and wished she could slow down the rapid thump-thump-thump of her heart. 'I...lost it.' She regretted hesitating over the choice of word to use, but she didn't want to implicate her brother. Not that Jago even knew she had a brother.

'Lost it or sold it?' Jago looked at her with a penetrating gaze she found a trifle unsettling. Suspicion lurked in his eyes, and it pained her to see it. She had lost his respect, and it stung. Oh, how it stung like acid poured into an open wound, her pride shrivelling, scarring.

Mollie had chosen not to tell Jago about her brother, not because she was ashamed of Eliot but because she had so skilfully whitewashed her background, simplifying it to make it less likely to trip over a lie. She had told Jago she was an only child, which was partially true—she was the only child of her mother and her scumbag of a father who hadn't bothered waiting around long enough for Mollie to be born. Eliot was her half-brother, the son of her mother and her mother's abusive partner, but to Mollie, there was nothing half about her love and concern for Eliot. He was her only living relative, and she was the only person he could rely on. Mollie had told Jago she was an orphan, which had created a connection with him at the time. The orphan bit wasn't a lie: her mother and her partner had both had drug and alcohol issues and ended their days in squalor, leaving two wild-eyed terrified children sitting with their decomposing bodies for three days before someone found them.

Mollie was no longer that pitiful six-year-old who hadn't been able to undo the deadbolt on the front door or open the painted-over latches on the windows. She was no longer without agency or control over her circumstances.

But Eliot...

Her heart tightened like it was in a cruel vice. Mollie hated thinking about how it had impacted his young brain, the neglect, the starvation, the drugs her mother's partner had given him to stop him crying... It seemed to her a betrayal of Eliot's privacy to tell everyone what had happened to him. Even he hadn't told her about the sexual abuse that had occurred in foster care until he was an adult. When Mollie started dating Jago, she'd realised his high profile would draw unwanted attention to her and then Eliot, if his existence became known. Who didn't love reading a salacious rags-to-riches story? It was clickbait on steroids. The headlines had flashed across her brain then, and they did so again now.

Impoverished Girl from the Wrong Side of the Tracks Engaged to Handsome Playboy Billionaire Jago Wilde

Drug-addicted Half-Brother with a Criminal Record Joins the Wealthy Wilde Family through Marriage

It was gut-churning to think of the damage it could have done—and still could do—to Eliot if he was exposed to unprincipled journalists hunting for a juicy story.

Mollie forced herself to hold Jago's laser beam gaze. 'I genuinely lost it. I have no idea where it is. I always intended to send it back to you. I'm sorry. I know it cost you a fortune and—'

'You're damn right it cost a fortune.' The bitterness in his voice was unmistakable, the scepticism in his gaze excoriating.

His vision of her as a gold-digger was understandable, but how could she change it without revealing her dark secrets? Secrets she wanted to keep hidden for her own benefit as well as Eliot's. Once she had reached the age of eighteen, she had changed her name to avoid being linked to that lice-infested, malnourished little girl with red welts on her legs from the savage beatings she had endured. She had distanced herself from little Margaret Green and become Mollie Cassidy.

Jago continued to look at her with his marble-hard gaze. 'I've already taken the liberty of purchasing a replacement ring. A fake one just in case you have any idea about—' he held up his fingers in air quotes '—*losing* it.'

Pride brought her chin up, and she held his gaze with gritty determination. 'I never asked you to buy me such a ridiculously expensive ring. It was a waste of money when there are homeless people on the streets.' Mollie knew she wasn't exactly following the gold-digger's handbook right now, but his distrust of her was so irritating. Fine for him with his mouthful of silver spoon to call her out on losing his priceless engagement ring.

But then to her horror, he reached inside his jacket pocket and took out a velvet ring box and set it on the table between them. He leaned back in his chair and surveyed her features with an inscrutable expression.

Mollie stared at the blue box, noticing it was almost the same colour as his eyes. She longed to reach for it but instead curled her fingers into her palms until she could feel the curve of her nails leaving crescent moon impressions in her skin.

'Go on. Take it. See if I got the size right.'

Mollie took a bracing breath and leaned forward to pick up the ring box. She waited a moment before lifting the lid, only just managing to block the rush of air that threatened to come past her lips in a hurricane gasp. It looked exactly the same as her lost ring. Only a jewellery expert would be able to prove it wasn't. The sapphire-and-diamond ring glittered at her, and she had trouble keeping her hand steady as she gazed at it with a host of memories flashing through her brain like a flicker tape movie. Jago's unexpected but romantic proposal the night he gave it to her. For someone who for most of her childhood had rarely received anything but charity shop gifts, Jago's choice of ring more than made up for it...or so she'd thought at the time. She remembered him sliding it over her knuckle, his fingers warm and gentle as they held her hand. She remembered his gaze focused on her with an intensity she hadn't seen in it before. And she remembered the overwhelming sense of joy, of feeling safe and secure for the first time in her life. She would have liked him to declare his love for her, but she'd fooled herself his proposal, his commitment, was enough. But of course, it wasn't. How could it have been?

'It won't bite your finger off if you put it on.' Jago's sardonic tone broke through her painful reverie.

Mollie flicked him a churlish glance and then took the ring out of the box, holding it up to the light to watch the diamonds catch the light from the chandelier overhead. 'It's a very convincing fake.'

'That's the plan—for you and the ring to be convincing fakes.'

Mollie still hadn't put the ring on but was holding it, wanting to accept his fake ring and fake fiancée offer but worried about the consequences; for there would be consequences, of that she was certain. Apart from facing Maxwell Wilde when he had banished her from his grandson's life forever, how could she spend a weekend in Jago's company without him tempting her all over again? She could feel the magnetic pull of him even now. He was the only man who had ever treated her with respect. His touch had sent tingles along her skin from the first moment they met. He had worshipped her body, taking it to heights it had never experienced before. Her skin came alive, her senses went into freefall, her need for him a powerful passionate drive she hadn't known she possessed until he'd awakened it in her.

'So you haven't told your grandfather of this plan of yours?'

'No.'

'But surely me suddenly turning up would be a terrible shock for him, wouldn't it?' Mollie had to be so careful with her words, so careful not to compromise the rules his grandfather had set down.

Jago gave a dismissive shrug of one broad shoulder. 'As I said before, he's not my primary concern right now, my grandmother is. She will be delighted to see you.' His eyes hardened a fraction, and he continued. 'She was heartbroken when our wedding was cancelled. I suspect that's why she doesn't remember it since her concussion—it was too painful for her.'

Mollie could feel the heat pooling in her cheeks and looked back down at the ring in the palm of her hand. It seemed to sit there mocking her with its glittering diamond eyes so like its giver. Daring her to put it on.

Come on. Do it. You know you want to.

She did want to, which was deeply troubling. She would be entering enemy territory, but she didn't know what Jago's grandfather would do. Would he accept her presence for the sake of his elderly and frail wife? Surely, he wouldn't be so cruel as to expose her past to Jago? But what about the AI-generated images? Maxwell had promised the images of her would go away, and since then two years had passed and she had begun to feel a tenuous sense of safety. He had stayed true to his word, so what would happen if she didn't keep her end of the deal? Maxwell had paid for her silence. He had paid her to go away. He had paid the blackmailer… She frowned and looked at the ring again, her thoughts spinning like clothes in a tumble dryer. Blackmailers didn't usually go away. They usually wanted more money once the first ransom was paid. They upped the ante, bleeding their victim to breaking point.

How had Maxwell Wilde got rid of them with a single payment? Or had he paid them more than he said? If so, it was even more brazen of her to reappear in his grandson's life. Mollie knew Jago wasn't close to his grandfather, but she also knew that blood was thicker than water and Wilde blood thicker than most because of their enormous wealth. Jago might well believe his grandfather over her version of events, and given how many lies she had told in the past, she could hardly blame him. She hadn't seen Jago the day she jilted him. He had been on his way back from New York, which made her look even more of a gold-digger for not having the decency to end their relationship in person. But Maxwell had insisted she leave before Jago got back. He had said it would be easier on everyone if she left, especially as the extortionist was threatening to make those wretched images go viral if the ransom wasn't paid within twelve hours. That looming deadline had made it impossible for Mollie to think things through with any sense of rationality. She had become almost like an automaton, a mindless puppet, doing everything Maxwell Wilde insisted she do. It made sense to her in her distressed and overwrought state to take up Maxwell's offer. It was an escape hatch she desperately needed. The money was not the only reason she left, although it was a part of it. A big part of it. She didn't want to bring shame on the man she loved. She didn't want to taint Jago with the dramas and traumas of her past. And she wanted to protect her brother who had no one else batting for him, believing in him that he could, with the right help, make something of his life before it was too late.

'Are you waiting for me to get down on bended knee or something?' Jago's voice had a note of mockery in it that stung like a slap.

Mollie flicked her gaze to his, doing everything

in her power to keep her expression cool and composed. 'Do you really think I'd be such a fool to accept a second time?'

A flash of incendiary heat lit Jago's gaze, and his mouth thinned. 'Who knows what you'd do if you could work it to your advantage? Why are you working in that clinic? I thought your dream was to set up your own luxury spa?'

Mollie had to control every muscle in her face so he didn't see how affected she was by the mention of her failed dream. She had fought so hard for so long, worked punishingly long hours and taken numerous courses to get the qualifications she needed to run her own day spa. But because of her brother's constant draining of her resources, she had been like Sisyphus pushing the ball up a steep hill, only to get within sight of the top for it to come rolling back down again, crushing her hopes and dreams. 'I still intend to open my own spa. It's taking a little longer than I planned, but I will hopefully get there in the end.'

Jago kept his gaze trained on hers. 'If you accept my offer, you can do it sooner rather than later.'

Mollie had already done the numbers in her head. With the amount Jago was offering, she could open her own spa and get Eliot the help he needed. She could achieve her life's dream, but by pretending to be engaged to Jago Wilde, she would have to live her worst nightmare. 'I need more time to think about this. It's a big decision and—'

'I want your answer now.' The implacable edge in

his tone reminded her she was the one with the most at stake. She wasn't in the position to bargain, to draw things out, to delay or stall to get time to measure the risks. Jago wanted a commitment now, and she would have to give it to him or lose this chance, this only chance, to save Eliot.

Mollie ran the tip of her tongue over the parched terrain of her lips. The supposed engagement ring she was holding in her palm was digging into her skin. Her stomach was churning with nerves, with dread, but also with a strange sense of excitement. The electric energy Jago generated in her made her think of how his hands had touched her, how his mouth had kissed her, how his body had entered her and taken her to paradise time and time again.

He was paying an exorbitant sum for her to pretend for the weekend of his grandmother's birthday, but would he expect more? Dare she ask what his intentions were? They would be in close contact, pretending to be the lovers they once were. How tempting would it be to slip into his arms, to reach for him, to consent to his earth-shattering lovemaking? Too tempting. Outrageously tempting. Every fibre of her being would have to fight the instinct, the raw and earthy drive to crush her mouth to his, to feel the sexy stroke of his tongue against hers, to wind her arms around his trim waist and pull his hardness against her softness. Thinking about it created a tumult of need in her lower body, her feminine core moistening with greedy want for the hard presence of his.

Jago's dark blue gaze glinted, and his sensual mouth lifted at the edges in a mercurial smile as if he was reading her mind as easily as reading an X-ray. 'If you're finding the prospect of sharing my room a little distasteful, let me assure you I will not lay a finger on you.'

Mollie swallowed a gasp of raw hurt that he no longer wanted her. Disappointment washed through her like a poison, making her fingertips fizz and her heart contract. But what else did she expect? She had jilted him the day before their wedding. She had not even explained why she had done it—she had left that to his grandfather. Jago no longer desired her; he now hated her and was intent on punishing her by making her play by his rules.

She wanted to reject his offer.

She wanted to stand up and throw her glass of water in his too handsome face.

She wanted to fist her hand in his crisp white shirt and pull his head down to press her mouth on his sensual one. To ignite the fire that was still smouldering between them. Flickers and flares of lust licked across her skin, blood pulsed and pounded in her feminine core, molten heat travelled to all her secret places simply by being in Jago Wilde's presence.

Mollie wanted him, and worst of all, she suspected he knew it.

Mollie decided to act like the gold-digger he believed her to be. It was born out of a perverse desire to retaliate, to hurt him as he had hurt her. She knew it was petty and immature of her, but she needed to shift the balance of power. For the sake of her pride, she couldn't allow him to toy with her like a string puppet, making her dance to whatever tune he chose to play. She would make him perform for her. And she knew exactly how to do it.

She knew her sensual power for he had awakened it in her, and it had bloomed and blossomed and blistered into an inferno. The heat between them still sparked in the atmosphere. She could see it reflected in the midnight blue of his gaze, could sense the tension in his toned body, could feel it thrumming in her own. A primitive beat of need that had not gone away in spite of her jilting him. He might say he wasn't interested in sleeping with her, but she knew his body. She knew the signs. She knew his taste, his touch, his smell, his wild and passionate need.

Mollie smiled to herself and crossed one slim leg over the other, holding his gaze without flinching. She would enjoy every moment of bringing Jago Wilde to his knees.

'All right, I accept your offer,' Mollie said.

If Jago was relieved she'd finally agreed to his plan, he didn't show any sign of it on his aristocratic features.

Mollie tried not to think about how little time she had to get herself prepared. She wouldn't only be seeing Elsie again but also Maxwell as well as Jago's brothers. They must all hate her by now. How could they not? She had embarrassed and humiliated their brother. She was a runaway bride, and even worse, she had accepted a significant sum of money to go away. She was reasonably sure Maxwell hadn't told the Wilde brothers the truth about why she had jilted Jago. Jago hadn't mentioned anything about the blackmailer and the AI images, so she assumed that was a detail about her deal with his grandfather he was not aware of, and hopefully it would stay that way. But blackmailers and money deals aside, Jago's brothers would be as appalled by her cowardly behaviour as she would be if the situation was reversed.

'Will your brothers be there?' Mollie asked, glancing at him.

Something moved at the back of Jago's eyes, a shadow, a flicker, a frozen nanosecond of internal thought before his vision cleared to its cold assessment of her. 'It will be a small gathering due to the fragile state of my grandmother's health. Jack will be there, but unfortunately Jonas can't be.'

'Oh, why not?'

'He's…abroad at present, working on an important project.' His slight hesitation before he explained his brother's absence made her sense something wasn't quite right.

'But I thought you told me once that Jonas is the closest of all of you to your grandmother? Why wouldn't he make the time to come and be with her, especially as you said her health is so fragile right now?'

Jago's expression became masked like curtains

closing over a stage. 'My grandmother will be disappointed, of course, but not offended by him not being there. She understands Jonas's work takes him abroad for months at a time. Besides, having you there with me will more than compensate for his absence. Her dream is to see at least one of her grandsons settled down before she passes.'

Mollie slid the ring over her finger, eyeing it like she was measuring its worth, but inside she was thinking *Can I really do this? Can I act convincingly enough?*

'There's another thing I need to stipulate,' Jago said. 'There is to be no talking to the press. I don't care how much you're offered for a tell-all interview, I forbid you to speak to them about our relationship, why it ended and why it's back on again.'

Mollie arched her eyebrows and lowered her hand to her lap. 'But it isn't back on again, is it? We're just pretending. Or do have plans to seduce me to get back at me for jilting you?'

A devilish glint appeared in his gaze. 'Now, there's a thought.' His eyes roved over her in a leisurely manner, causing her body to flare with molten heat.

Mollie knew he was thinking of all the times he had stripped her naked, all the times he had kissed her body from head to toe. All the times he had possessed her, gently, roughly, urgently, passionately. She wasn't one to blush readily, but she could feel the hot bloom of colour flowing into her cheeks once more as each erotic memory flooded her brain. Blood flowed to her inner core, making her feminine folds swell with wicked want. How could she control this driving need for him? Was it because she had been celibate for two years? Even her breasts tingled inside the lace of her cheap bra, as if anticipating the roll of his tongue, the warm, wet suck of his mouth, the sexy scrape of his teeth and the rasp of his stubble on her soft flesh. He could unravel her senses, blow her mind and her body just by looking at her. She would have to be careful how she handled him this coming weekend. It had broken her heart to give him up two years ago; she wasn't sure she would survive a second time.

Mollie challenged him with her gaze, using every bit of acting talent she had gained over the years of her crazy, chaotic life. 'If you put one finger on me, Jago Wilde, I will make you regret it.'

Jago gave a mocking laugh that grated on her already shredded nerves. Then he leaned forward, his forearms resting on his muscular thighs, his eyes nailing hers. Even though there was a coffee table between them, it seemed like no distance at all. This close, she could see the individual pinpricks of his dark stubble that liberally peppered his jaw. Her fingers itched to run over his skin, to feel the abrasion of his growth on her softer skin. She suppressed a tiny shiver and tried to stop thinking of what it had been like to have his head between her legs, his tongue playing her like a maestro plays a priceless instrument. Why couldn't she forget all the times he had touched her? The memories were burned, seared, scorched into her flesh like a brand.

'We will have to act like lovers while we're at Wildewood Manor. You will have to accept my touch, even my kisses, or the deal is off. Understood?' His voice was deep and gravel-rough and underlined with the implacability she knew was an essential part of his personality.

Feminist she might be, but his unshakable authority sent a delicate frisson over her flesh. She had locked horns with him in the past, and it had always been resolved with smoking-hot sex. Make-up sex. But there was no way Jago would ever forgive her for jilting him, so any sex between them now would be revenge sex.

Could she allow her body to be used that way? But her body still craved him, so how would it be anything but a mutual explosion of the senses? Jago wanted her on his terms, but she had terms of her own and she would insist on them.

Mollie ground her teeth behind her painted smile. 'I want to be paid up-front.'

Cynicism burned in his gaze like a laser beam. 'That can be arranged, but it comes with conditions.'

A feather of unease danced up and down her spine. 'What conditions?'

'You've run away from me before. I am not letting it happen again.'

'I promise you I won't—'

'Your promises mean nothing to me. They are

worthless,' Jago said in a harsh tone that lashed her like the flick of a whip. His eyes were so dark they were almost blue-black, and his jaw was tight as a clamp.

And yet again, her traitorous body revelled in his commanding manner. It made every cell of her body tingle with awareness and every inch of her skin tighten. Even though he clearly hated her, Mollie knew without a doubt he still wanted her. It was written in his features, it pulsed like electricity in the atmosphere, it circled back and forth between them like a fizzing current. It gave her a fraction of power in their relationship as it stood now. Physical power she could use to her advantage. And she would use it. She would be as ruthless as she needed to be to survive being around him again.

'It's only Wednesday,' Mollie pointed out. 'You can hardly keep me chained to your side until Friday.'

One black brow arched up in a satirical manner. 'Can't I?'

Another frisson of excitement coursed. He was ruthless enough to do whatever it took to get what he wanted, especially now. He was a Wilde, and the name was synonymous with *ruthlessness*.

What Wilde men wanted, they got.

'I'll come with you Friday, but I need time to prepare myself,' Mollie said. 'We've spent two years apart. It won't be easy to slip back into the role of your fiancée.'

Jago leaned back in his chair, one of his hands

scraping his hair back from his face, leaving deep fingertip grooves in the thick black strands. How many times had she lain draped across his naked body, her fingers doing the very same thing to his hair? Was he remembering it? Remembering how it felt to hold her, to possess her? She studied his expression, searching for a clue to what he was feeling, but all she could see was bitterness and distrust etched in his handsome features. It pained her to think of what their relationship could have been if it hadn't been for those dreadful photos of her.

They might have even had a baby by now...

They hadn't discussed having children in much detail, but she knew it was Jago's grandmother's yearning desire to hold a great-grandchild in her arms before she died. Neither of Jago's brothers were settled down, although Mollie had seen a gossip article about Jonas and his girlfriend, Tessa Macclesfield, who he had dated for a couple of months. Coincidentally, Tessa was the wedding cake designer who had designed Mollie and Jago's spectacular wedding cake. Mollie had always wanted to call on Tessa and apologise in person at her shop in Notting Hill, but there hadn't been time before she'd left to move to Scotland to get Eliot into a private rehab clinic in Glasgow. He had left after four months, which had been heartbreaking for her. Heartbreaking to have a glimpse of hope only for it to be snatched away again. But he had agreed to try it again and had been there six months so far this time. But it was expensive. Hideously, terrifyingly expensive for someone in Mollie's dire financial position. The money Jago was offering would not only pay for a whole year or more of private rehab but could also get her started in her own health and beauty spa. To have her brother healed as well as her career on track was like wishing for the moon and stars and the International Space Station, but she refused to give up hope. If she gave up on her dream, then she would have failed herself as well as her brother.

'I have a few business things to see to in Edinburgh tomorrow, but we will fly down to London early on Friday then drive to Wildewood,' Jago said. 'Give me your address so I can pick you up on Friday.' He took out his phone in preparation to type in her current address.

Mollie gave him a quizzical look. 'But surely you must already know it. I mean, you found my clinic easily enough. Did you engage the services of a private investigator to track me down?'

Jago lowered his phone to look at her. 'You once mentioned you'd always wanted to visit Scotland. I did a little research and found out a young woman matching your description was working in a beauty clinic here.'

Mollie wouldn't put it past him to have engaged MI5 to track her down. There were numerous beauty clinics in Edinburgh and its surrounds. But then, Jago had connections most people could only dream about. Wilde money opened doors and created opportunities way out of reach for the general population. But it was a little unnerving to think it hadn't taken Jago long to find her. She wondered if he already knew about her awful little bedsit and was only asking for her address as a formality. Again, it made her think of how she could have been living in the lap of luxury if she hadn't jilted him two years ago. She certainly wouldn't be living in a cramped and mould-ridden studio on the basement floor of a rundown tenement house.

Mollie told him her address, keeping her expression masked as he typed it in his phone. She looked at his long fingers as he entered her address, her imagination taking her places she knew she shouldn't be going. Those fingers had touched her, stroked her, tantalised her in places no one else had touched. She could not imagine wanting anyone else to touch her now even though two long, lonely years had passed. Her body was branded by his touch, her mouth craved only his taste, and she couldn't see it changing anytime soon.

Jago Wilde, damn him, had quite literally ruined her for anyone else.

CHAPTER THREE

JAGO WAS RELUCTANT to let Mollie out of his sight, but short of kidnapping her, there was nothing he could do but escort her home and hope she didn't do a runner before Friday. Being with her again stirred up so many emotions, none of which he wanted to acknowledge. He had never considered himself a jealous man, but since meeting Mollie, he had seen the way other men looked at her. With her long light brown hair and grey-blue eyes, she could easily have graced the cover of a high fashion magazine. She moved with a ballerina's grace, floating, gliding, ethereal. Her face was a neat oval, her nose a ski slope, her mouth… Oh God, why did he have to keep looking at her mouth? His own lips tingled with the memory of the softness of her lips against his. His lower body turned to steel as he recalled those lips sucking on him. Even their first kiss had detonated something inside him, sending him wild with need. A need that had reawakened by being in her presence. Since their break-up, he had not rushed into a new relationship but left it for close to a year before he ventured back to his playboy lifestyle. Strangely, it hadn't satisfied him the way it had before, which he was reluctant to admit to anyone, including himself. The press made a big deal about his enviable lifestyle—wealthy, privileged, with his choice of women to entertain him as he pleased.

But since Mollie had left him, no one pleased him.

Jago had accumulated even more wealth in the two years since the cancelled wedding, but he didn't take any pride or satisfaction in the extra millions in his bank account and property and investment portfolio. He didn't feel any sense of pride in what he had achieved. Instead, he felt a sense of niggling failure that the one person he wanted had got away. Had got away because she had valued money over him.

That was something he could not forgive.

Jago looked across at Mollie sitting with a cool and untouchable expression on her face. She could be so animated when they discussed something she was passionate about, and yet at other times, she could shut down her features in a blink of her eyes, effectively locking him out like a window shutter. Like any couple, they had had their differences of opinion at times, but their electric physical chemistry had always ironed out those differences with a distracting lovemaking session. And they had been spectacularly distracting. So distracting, he still could not erase them from his mind. If he allowed himself, he would think about her skin against his every day. He had never been the type of man to obsess over a lover. He had flings, so many flings he had trouble recalling faces, let alone names. When a fling was over, it was over. Never had he ruminated on a break-up like his with Mollie. But then, he hadn't broken up with her—she had done it to him and in the most humiliating way of all.

But in spite of all that, Mollie had somehow burrowed her way into his brain and body to the point he was nearly always thinking about her, and that *had* to change. He had to move on, and his grandmother's recent memory loss had given him the perfect way to do it.

It occurred to him he didn't know how to reach Mollie other than physically. That had been their language, their communication. A look, a kiss, a stroke of a finger, a hand down the other's face or arm had spoken volumes. His body pounding into her welcoming silky wetness had told him all he needed to know…back then.

Now, with her sitting coldly and closed off from him with a coffee table as a barrier between them, Jago realised he knew nothing of her life over the last two years. What had she done with the money his grandfather had paid her to go away? It was a significant sum and yet she was working in a rundown suburb in a beauty clinic that looked like it needed more of a makeover than its clients. He had only found out about the money in the last few months as he had taken over more and more of his grandfather's business affairs. His grandfather's stroke a year ago had not just affected his physical mobility, but Maxwell no longer had the sharpness of intellect one needed to run a multi-arm corporation. Jago had his own property development business to run, but at least he had the skills and mental acuity to juggle both businesses, although it was tough right now with his younger brother, Jonas, out of the country for an unspecified time. While Jonas occasionally went off-grid to work as a naval architect on top-secret missions, his sudden departure seven months ago had been a little unusual. Not that Jago was close with either of his brothers—their grandfather had seen to that—but Jonas was the closest to their grandmother. Jago hadn't even been able to get a message through to him about their gran's health crisis. Jonas had simply disappeared, leaving instructions that no one was to contact him, including the young woman he had been dating. But that was his younger brother's personal business. Jago had his own to sort out.

'So what have you been doing with yourself the last two years?' Jago asked to break the silence because it was becoming obvious to him Mollie was not going to.

Mollie's eyes dipped to the glass she was holding, the ice cubes rattling against the sides. 'Working.'

'Because you want to or you need to?'

Mollie gave him an unreadable glance. 'Both.'

He had trouble controlling the urge to curl his lip. 'It didn't take you long to get rid of the money my grandfather paid you. What did you do with it?'

Her small chin came up, and her eyes flashed like

a struck match. 'I am not going to discuss my financial affairs with you.' Her tone could have clipped a yew hedge.

Jago held her gaze with iron determination. 'Ah yes, the non-disclosure agreement.' It was a guess on his part, but Jago knew enough about his grandfather to realise Maxwell would never leave himself open for exploitation. No way would he pay someone off without making sure they never told anyone about it. For as long as Jago could remember, the press had feasted on stories of the Wilde brothers. Jago's grandfather was, in his halcyon days, a savvy businessman who had used every means in the book to build his wealth, not necessarily for his family but for the sake of his ego and overblown pride. But since his stroke, his grandfather had had to rely on Jago to take over more and more responsibility, a situation Maxwell did not accept with grace or gratitude but with criticism and grumpiness.

Mollie's eyes flared for the briefest moment at the mention of the non-disclosure agreement, but she didn't respond. She swirled the contents of her glass, then lifted it to her lips and took a measured sip. He got the sense she was trying to find her way through a verbal minefield, careful in what she said and how she said it. She put the glass back on the table between them with almost exaggerated precision, then sat back and met his gaze with a cool stare that made him all the more determined to get under her fortresslike guard.

'I know what my grandfather is capable of,' Jago said into the throbbing silence. 'He's ruthless and manipulative and will stop at nothing to get what he wants.'

Mollie's neat eyebrows rose ever so slightly, and her mouth slanted at a cynical angle. 'You could easily be describing yourself, coming all this way with offers of money to get me to do what you want.'

Jago had to stop himself from clenching his jaw out of frustration. Of course he was prepared to be ruthless. He had to be to get her to come to his grandmother's birthday, and he would do whatever it took to achieve it. He didn't trust her not to do another runner on him, so he had to find a way to keep her close, as dangerous as that was. Dangerous because of the sexual chemistry that still thrummed in the air between them. He could feel it in his body—the stirring of his blood, the swelling and tightening of his flesh as he recalled the way she'd welcomed him into her body in the past. Had she really wanted him back then, or had it all been an act? She had been so damned convincing he had fallen for it. Fallen hard. Not in love, but in lust. Red-hot and flaming. Lust so powerfully addictive he had never wanted it to end, thus the marriage proposal. It was the one thing he prided himself on—that he hadn't told her he loved her.

She had said those three little words, albeit in a whisper one night after making love, but he hadn't said them back. He had pretended to be asleep, for saying those words were difficult for him because the last time he told someone he loved them—his parents—they didn't come back. Not that he truly believed he had been in love with her anyway, or at least he didn't want to think he had been that foolish to fall in love with someone who threw him over for money. It was physical attraction that had bound him to her back then. Their connection had reminded him of his parents' strong physical bond: they had been so happy with each other until fate stepped in and ruined everything.

'Money seems to be the only thing that appeals to you,' Jago said, nailing her with his gaze.

'Money has universal appeal, does it not?' Her voice was straight out of the gold-digger's playbook but something about her eyes reminded him of a wrong note played in a performance.

Jago reached into his jacket pocket for a single-sheet document. He unfolded it and handed it to her.

'What's that?'

'A contract.'

She stared at it for a moment before taking it with a hand that was not quite steady. She drew it closer and scanned it with her gaze, her teeth momentarily snagging her lower lip. Then she released her lower lip and looked at him in a guarded manner. 'You want me to sign this?'

'Of course.'

She glanced back at the sheet of paper in her hand, but he had a feeling it wasn't to reread the contract written there but rather as a way to avoid his gaze. Her jaw worked for a moment like she was clenching her jaw to control her emotions. Then she lifted her gaze back to his, her mouth in a line so tight her lips were almost white. 'You're way more like your grandfather than I thought.'

Jago acknowledged her comment with a wry smile. 'I'm not sure he would agree with you. He's made it his life's work to toughen my brothers and me up.'

'It's clearly worked.' There was a stinging note to her voice, and it pleased him to have got under her skin.

Jago lifted one shoulder in a careless shrug. 'I'm tough when I need to be.' He took out his gold pen and handed it to her. 'Sign the contract between us. I'll get the money to you first thing tomorrow.'

Mollie took the pen from him with another gelid glare. 'I'm not signing until I have the money.'

Jago ground his back teeth and mentally apologised to his dentist for the damage he was probably doing. 'I'm not handing over a penny until you sign. Take it or leave it.'

Mollie flicked the pen back and forth between her fingers, looking as if she'd rather use it as a weapon. 'You don't trust me, do you?'

'Nope.'

If she was wounded by his response she didn't show it. Instead, she leaned forward to put the paper on the coffee table, then signed the contract with a flourish, before handing both the pen and paper back to him. 'You can transfer the funds into my back account right here and now. I'll text you the details.' She sat back and took her phone out of her purse and texted him her details.

Jago's phone pinged a few seconds later, and he swiped the screen open to view her message. 'I'll give you half now and the rest at the end of the weekend.'

'But you said you'd—'

'It's in the contract you just signed.'

Mollie gestured with her fingers for him to hand the contract back to her. He did so, and she scrutinised it like a forensic detective. Her mouth tightened, and her gaze blazed, and she handed the contract back. 'Fine. Half now, the rest later.'

Jago opened his banking app on his phone and transferred the funds. There was no way he was going to let her out of his sight, contract or not. He pushed back his sleeve to glance at his watch then brought his gaze back to hers. 'It's getting late.' He stood and, scooping the now empty ring box off the coffee table, handed it to her. She took it with a scowl and opened her purse and dropped it inside, clicking it shut with a snap.

'Come on,' he said. 'I'll escort you home.'

Mollie rose to her feet with regal grace, but her eyes were on still on fire. 'That is totally unnecessary. I can find my own way home.'

'I'm sure you can, but I have a burning desire to see where you live.' He had another burning desire, one he wished he could switch off, but his body wouldn't obey the rational commands of his brain. It had its own agenda, and it was making it hard for him to imagine getting through the next few minutes without touching her, let alone sharing a bedroom at Wildewood Manor this coming weekend.

Mollie had no choice but to do as Jago commanded. Even she could see the sense in Jago making sure he knew where she lived since he had just handed over a veritable fortune. But allowing him to see her ghastly little bedsit was the ultimate in humiliation, especially when he knew she had already been given a large sum of money by his grandfather. Still, she was supposed to be playing the gold-digger, so she would have to act like a pro to get through it. She followed Jago out of the swish hotel bar and stood by his side as he used a rideshare app. Normally, she walked or caught public transport, but it had started raining, and even though it was spring, the Edinburgh air was bracing to say the least. She tucked her evening purse under one arm and cupped her elbows with her hands in an effort to keep warm. She had lived in Edinburgh long enough to know how capricious the weather could be. But the only warm coat she possessed was so old and unfashionable she had decided against bringing it with her.

'You're shivering.'

'I'm n-not.'

Jago shrugged himself out his jacket and then draped it across her shoulders. The warmth of his jacket suddenly enveloped her, intoxicating her with his body heat as well as his spicy cologne. Her nostrils flared to take in more of that alluring smell evoking such sizzling erotic memories that even the ice-cold rain couldn't cool down.

Mollie glanced up at him. 'Aren't you cold?'

He gave a crooked smile that sent a dart to her heart. 'I'm tough, remember?'

The rideshare pulled up in front of them at that moment, which saved Mollie the necessary brainpower to think of a witty reply. He opened the door for her and she got in, sweeping the skirt of her dress inside the car with her hand. He closed the door and got in the other side, greeting the driver with a polite exchange of words, before clipping his seatbelt in place.

Jago met her gaze, and she watched as his eyes drifted to her mouth. 'Thawed out yet?'

'Getting there.' Mollie wasn't entirely sure he was talking about the weather. She knew she had to pretend to be engaged to him in front of his grandmother, which meant she could hardly act cold and indifferent towards him. Her eyes went to his mouth seemingly of their own volition, and her heart skipped a beat. How was she going to act cold and indifferent when he looked at her like that? His eyes darkened to the colour of the night sky. The focus in them was intense as if he was imagining the press of her lips against his and the meeting of their tongues. She shivered and hugged his jacket closer, forcing her gaze to look in the direction of travel.

Mollie had always known Jago was tough, but he

definitely seemed even tougher now. More ruthless. More determined to get his way. Had she done that to him by jilting him? He hadn't been in love with her, so it wasn't as if she had broken his heart. She had dented his pride more than anything else. But now her pride was at stake as the rideshare took them closer to her bedsit. Her heart rate increased as the car rumbled over every cobblestone on the back streets that looked even more dismal and dangerous in the growing darkness and driving rain.

A short time later, the driver pulled up outside her address. Jago got out and came around to her side of the car before she had even undone her seatbelt. Something with small, pointed teeth was nibbling at her stomach lining, and her heart was pumping like she had just run up the steps of the Scott Monument.

Jago opened her door and did his best to shield her from the pelting rain. He thanked the driver and then closed the car door. Mollie held his jacket over her head and dashed to the steps that led to her lower-ground flat. She didn't need to look at Jago's face to witness his disgust at her accommodation as he followed her down the stone steps. She summoned up the remnants of her pride and took out her keys from her purse and unlocked the door, stepping inside and handing him back his jacket. 'I'm sorry it's so wet. Thank you for the lift home.'

He took the jacket from her and hung it on a hook on the back of the door then closed it. He turned and gave the room an assessing sweep with his gaze, his mouth tightening. 'This is your home?' His incredulous tone was another dent to her pride, the derision in his gaze making her cheeks burn.

Mollie raised her chin, determined to stand her ground with him. She had lived in worse. Much worse. 'Careful, Jago, you'll wake the neighbours speaking with all those silver spoons dangling from your mouth.'

He rolled his eyes at her attempt at humour, but his mouth was still in a tight line. 'How long have you been living here?' His ink-black eyebrows were drawn into a severe frown making him look intimidating but concerned at the same time.

'I've only been here a few months.' Mollie shook back her hair, determined not to show how embarrassed she was at him seeing how far she had fallen. She had had so few choices when it came to accommodation after Eliot's rehabilitation deposit took the rest of her savings. She had missed meals and turned off the heating in order to get through. It certainly wasn't how she'd expected her life to turn out. She had done everything possible to avoid living in the same squalor as her mother and stepfather, but Eliot's problems made it difficult for her to get ahead. She was unfortunately casually employed at the clinic, which meant she could be told by her employer to stay home if not enough clients had booked in on any particular day. She literally did not know from one week to the next how much money she might earn.

But you have plenty of money now.

Mollie was tempted to open her banking app on her phone just to see the money in her account that Jago had transferred earlier. If she could get through the coming weekend with him at his grandmother's birthday party, she wouldn't need to return to the beauty clinic at all. She could set up her own business in a nicer area. Her flagging dream took in a deep lungful of air, inflating Mollie's hopes to the point where she began to feel light-headed and giddy with the possibility of success at last.

Jago proceeded to do an inspection of her flat like he was some sort of structural engineer. His expression grew all the more thunderous as he tapped against the walls and turned the tiny kitchen's taps on and off. Mollie folded her arms and watched him with a bored teenager look on her face.

Finally, he turned and faced her. 'You're not staying here another minute.'

She arched her brows in an imperious manner. 'Excuse me?'

He blew out an impatient breath—one with a thick curse word attached on its backdraft. 'You can't possibly live like this. It's practically a hovel.'

'I've lived in far worse.' Mollie could have bitten off her tongue as soon as the words were out. She had told Jago nothing of her chaotic and disadvantaged childhood. She had removed all trace of her past, changing her name and her accent in order to take herself as far away from it as possible. And she had mostly done so...except Eliot kept pulling her back like a towrope she could not and would not sever.

Jago's blue eyes narrowed, his frown forming two deep pleats between his eyebrows. 'Worse?' His voice had a probing quality to it. He reminded Mollie of a detective who had picked up a significant detail of evidence everyone else had missed.

'Not everyone grows up in an Elizabethan manor house with its own country park, Jago. Not everyone flies in private jets for their holidays or has chauffeurs driving them to and from boarding school each term,' Mollie said with scorn dripping from every word. Or maybe it was jealousy. Who wouldn't be jealous of the Wilde lifestyle?

'Yeah, and not everyone loses their parents in a plane crash when they're five years old,' Jago said with a thickness in his voice she had never heard in it before. 'No amount of money or property can compensate for that.'

There was a silence so intense only the sound of the kitchen tap's leak could be heard. *Plop... Plop... Plop...*

Mollie had never heard him mention his parents before. She had read about the light-plane crash that had tragically killed his father and mother, but she had never heard Jago refer to them. Not once, even though she had been engaged to him, shared his bed, his life, his world. She hadn't pushed him to talk about them because she had ghosts of her own she preferred to keep well hidden.

But it was her scornful words now that had triggered him to speak of his heartbreaking loss, and she was ashamed of herself. Deeply ashamed. It was a cheap shot and cruel of her, given all she knew about being an orphan. Yes, he'd been fortunate enough to have grandparents to step in and raise him and his brothers, but Mollie had good cause to wonder if Maxwell Wilde had been an ideal parent substitute. She thought of Jago, the middle of the Wilde brothers, only five years old. Old enough to know what had happened and to feel gut-wrenching grief and despair, and yet so young, so terribly young.

Mollie swallowed against a stricture in her throat. 'I'm sorry...' She moistened her dry lips and continued in a scratchy voice. 'You're absolutely right. No amount of money could ever make up for such a tragic loss.'

Jago moved back to the kitchen sink and tightened the tap until there were no more drips. 'That should stop it for now.'

So there was to be no acknowledgement of her apology and no further conversation about his parents. But Mollie could sense the tension in him, the tightness of his expression and the shadows in his eyes hinting at deeply suppressed emotions.

'But I won't be able to turn it on again,' Mollie said, glancing at the tap he had just tightened.

An implacable look came into his eyes. 'You won't be turning that tap on again. You're coming with me. Now.'

Mollie's eyes widened in alarm. 'Now?'

'Go pack a bag. There's no way I'm allowing you to come back here. Not even after the weekend.'

'But I have a lease that's—'

'I'll sort out the lease.'

Mollie's pride brought her chin up to a defiant height. 'What gives you the right to tell me where I can live?'

He took her left hand in his and held it up so the fake engagement ring glinted. 'This.'

Mollie snatched in a breath at the feel of his fingers wrapped around hers. His hold was gentle, and yet she suspected if she pulled away, he would tighten his grip. But strangely, she didn't want to pull away. She was a tiny iron filing, and he was a powerful magnet, drawing her closer, closer, closer. She could feel her heart rate pick up, a hectic pace that made her feel dizzy. Or maybe that was because she was only a few centimetres from his rock-hard chest and strongly muscled thighs. The desire to close the gap was almost unbearable, every muscle and sinew in her body wanted to feel him against her. All of him. Her body recognised him, the heat and smell of him, the strength and power of him an aphrodisiac she had no immunity against.

'We both know that's just a fake ring,' Mollie said, trying but failing to stop from glancing at his mouth.

His mouth kicked up at one corner in a wry smile, his eyes sexily hooded as his gaze drifted to her lips. 'That may not be real, but this is, isn't it?' And his mouth came down to just above hers, hovering there as if he knew every cell in her body was throbbing with the need to feel his lips against hers.

'I don't know what you're talking about.' Mollie tried to keep her voice even but her increasing breathing rate betrayed her. It was so damn hard to resist him. Her lips were tingling with anticipation, her legs feeling as if the bones had turned to liquid. She still hadn't pulled her hand out of his, still hadn't stepped back from the scorching temptation of his masculine body that called out to her with a primitive energy she could feel in her most feminine flesh.

'I think you do.' His mouth came even closer, his warm minty breath wafting across her lips, making them tingle all the more. 'You want me to kiss you, to see if the magic is still there.'

Ironic that he should speak of magic for Mollie's eyelids lowered like she was being cast under a spell. Her senses were intoxicated by his proximity, every cell of her body aching for him to crush her mouth beneath his. She swept the tip of her tongue over her lips, her heart kicking like a wild animal against her breastbone, her body tilting towards him as if she had no power to stop it. But then she didn't. Jago Wilde was her kryptonite: he could get her to do anything with the sensual power he had over her. She gave him an upwards glance to see the glinting intent in his midnight blue gaze. Something tilted sideways in her stomach like a bowl of liquid threatening to spill over. Moist heat throbbed between her thighs, and she closed the distance between their bodies, her breasts pushed up against his chest, her free hand going to the front of his shirt, fisting in it to bring his mouth down to hers.

CHAPTER FOUR

MOLLIE DIDN'T CARE THAT she had let him win by making her reveal her desire for him. Right then, all she cared about was the feel of his lips moving on hers with such explosive sensual heat. His mouth was firm and yet gentle, cajoling her into joining a dance as old as time itself.

But this was *their* dance, the sexy tango that she had only ever experienced with this degree of pleasure with Jago. His lips moulded to hers as if they had been crafted for exactly this purpose, to tease hers into sensual play and transport her to another place, a place where nothing mattered but the molten heat that fizzed and flashed and fired between them. Their chemistry hadn't changed: if anything, there was a new quality to it. A desperate clawing sort of hunger because they both knew this was not going to last forever. By the end of the weekend, they would return to their separate lives. Somehow that made their kiss all the more passionate, even poignant.

Jago's hands went to her hips, holding her against his hardened body, his mouth moving with mind-blowing expertise on hers. He made a guttural sound and deepened the kiss with a bold stroke of his tongue. Mollie couldn't hold back her own sounds of pleasure and encouragement, her tongue dancing with his in an erotic choreography that sent tingles racing up and down her spine. How had she gone without Jago's kisses for two years? How had she denied herself the sensual pleasure of being hotly wanted, urgently desired by a full-blooded man? But what other man could ever make her feel this way? Jago was the only man who had ever made her feel this level of arousal, this level of enjoyment, this level of delight.

Jago finally lifted his mouth off hers and looked down at her with desire shining like a bright light in his eyes. His hands were still on her hips, his arousal pressing against her stomach. Her own arousal was pulsing away in silky secrecy, a throbbing ache, a sense of being left hanging. But she tried not to show it in her face. She didn't want him to know how close she was to begging him to make love to her here and now. To satisfy the ache, to ease the burning fire of her longing. She was conscious of his gaze scanning her face, his expression inscrutable all except for the glitter of unrelieved desire in his eyes.

Mollie moved out of his hold and smoothed her dress over her hips, giving him a worldly glance that was a million miles from what she was really feeling. 'If you kiss me like that in public, people will think you're madly in love with me.'

'Don't go confusing lust with love,' he said with one of his trademark cynical smiles.

'I'm not going to make that mistake twice,' Mollie said with an edge of bitterness she couldn't eradicate in time. 'You weren't in love with me, so why you asked me to marry you in the first place is a total mystery to me.'

His features hardened like fast-setting concrete. 'There's no mystery about why you said *yes*, though, is there? You would never have accepted my proposal if I'd been some regular guy with a basic income. You saw money and fell in love with that, not me.'

Mollie held his stony look with enormous self-possession, a skill she had perfected since childhood. 'I think it's time you left.'

'Not without you.' Thunder rumbled in his voice, and lightning flashed in his gaze.

She arched her brows and folded her arms in an intractable pose. 'You're not the boss of me.' She knew she sounded like a recalcitrant child, but his overbearing manner was getting her riled up. That was another power he had over her: he could make her lose control of her carefully crafted self-possession in a heartbeat.

Jago drew in a slow breath and released it in a steady stream. His shoulders loosened, and his features softened as if he was trying to calm himself down. He moved over to the other side of the room and sat on the worn sofa, his left arm draped languidly across the back. 'I'll wait here until you pack what you need for the next two nights and the weekend.'

Mollie wanted to argue the point with him, but she thought of the huge sum of money he had already paid her and the remaining balance she would receive at the end of the weekend. She would be every type of fool not to do as he said. She hated her bedsit anyway. Why make such a big deal out of something she would gladly escape for a few days? She, too, blew out a long breath and dropped her tense shoulders. 'I'm not sleeping with you. I want to make that clear right here and now.' Mollie was saying it more for her own benefit than his. She had to resist him. She had to find a way to break his powerful, sensual spell over her.

'You're under no obligation to sleep with me. We do, however, have to appear in public as if we are an engaged couple, so that will require some display of affection from time to time.'

Mollie steeled her spine, holding his unreadable gaze with an effort. 'There's one thing that concerns me...' She unfolded her arms and let out another breath, wondering if she should risk mentioning his grandfather. She dared not reveal the reason why she took the money and ran, but she was concerned about seeing Maxwell when he had expressly told her never to contact Jago again. To turn up at Wildewood Manor newly reunited with Jago was going to cause a mountain of a trouble she could do without. What if Maxwell decided to punish her by leaking the images of her for reneging on their deal? But then Mollie thought of Elsie, Jago's grandmother who, because of her memory loss, still believed her grandson was engaged. And then there was the money Jago had paid her to pretend to be his fiancée. She could not do without that money because it was her last chance to help her brother. She might never get another opportunity to get Eliot the help he so desperately needed. She had failed him before; she would not do so again. If she had to risk a scandal if those deepfakes were released, then so be it. Jago knew she had been paid to go away, but as far as she could tell, he didn't know why she had accepted the payment. He assumed she was a gold-digger and had planned the whole thing, to pretend to fall in love with him and run away as soon as she got a payout.

'If you're worried about my grandfather, don't be,' Jago said. 'He doesn't have the power he used to have. He'll grumble and insult you like he does everyone, but he can't force you to stay away. Anyway, we're only going to be there two nights.'

Mollie scratched at the inside of her wrist, a nervous habit she had when stressed. 'But what if your grandmother doesn't get her memory back? Won't you have to tell her we're not engaged then?'

Jago rose from the sofa in one fluid movement, his hand raking through the thick pelt of his hair, a frown pulling at his brow. 'She's very frail since the fall. The doctors aren't giving any guarantees about her prognosis. She may live weeks or months, no one knows. My grandfather's stroke last year put extra stress on her, even though we employed help with his care. She tried to take care of him herself, and he, of course, has not been an easy patient.'

'It must be hard facing the prospect of losing your grandmother. I mean, she raised you and your brothers since your parents' death.'

There was a cavernous silence.

Jago's jaw worked for a moment, his eyes moving away from hers to look past her left shoulder as if he was looking into the past, remembering the day of the plane crash and how the news was broken to him. Mollie could see the flickering emotions going through his gaze like a reel of memories. But then he blinked a couple of times and met her eyes again. 'I'll give you ten minutes to pack your bag. We'll spend tonight at my hotel and then travel to Wildewood tomorrow instead of Friday. I think it's best if we get down there sooner rather than later.'

'But I have to tell my boss I'm not coming in and—'

'Is it your dream job?'

'No.'

'Do you like your boss?'

Mollie grimaced. 'Not particularly.'

'Then, you can hand in your notice by email or phone call. The money I gave you will tide you over for a year without having to work.'

But it won't tide me over when most of it is going towards getting help for Eliot.

Of course, she didn't tell Jago that. 'I have clients booked in for tomorrow,' Mollie said, even though she only had one the last time she'd looked, and they might well have cancelled by now anyway. But she had to find a chance to talk to Eliot in private to tell him she was going away for the weekend. She only hoped he would stay at the rehab clinic long enough for his cycle of addiction to be broken.

'Fine,' Jago said. 'But as soon as you're finished, I'll pick you up, and we'll head straight to the airport.'

Mollie left him to go and pack her bag, her thoughts in turmoil. Being in proximity with Jago for the next few days would test her resolve in ways it had never been tested before. She had to resist the temptation to fall into bed with him, but their kiss had shown her how weak her defences were. His kiss had reawakened her desire for him, the driving need that had drawn her to him two years ago. Lust was the way he described his feelings for her, but she knew deep in her bones that it was more than that for her. She had developed feelings for him in the few short months they had dated and become engaged. She would not have agreed to marry him unless she had genuinely loved him. She had spent the last two years trying to forget about him, trying to fool herself she no longer loved him, but that passionate kiss had shown her what dangerous territory she was venturing into again. Her heart had never quite healed from having to jilt him. To turn her back on the future she had dreamed of with him had cost her dearly emotionally. But what else could she have done? If those ghastly images had gone viral, she would have been publicly shamed and vilified, not to mention humiliated beyond imagination. Jago's reputation, too, would have been sullied by his association with her. Maxwell Wilde might well be a hard-nosed businessman with a ruthless streak wider than the English Channel, but she knew he would do anything and everything to protect the Wilde name. Mollie had no idea how Maxwell was going to react when he saw her with Jago this coming weekend. Jago didn't seem to be too concerned, but how much did he know? If his grandfather had told him about the images, surely Jago wouldn't be inviting her back into his life, even if it was only for a weekend of playing at being engaged?

Jago paced the floor in Mollie's bedsit like a lion in a cat carrier. Why was she living in such a rundown place? The money she had been paid by his grandfather should have been enough to set her up better than this. She could have bought a nice apartment, even a nice house in a genteel suburb. What had she done with the money? Did she have a gambling problem? Did she do drugs? It seemed highly unlikely for she didn't even drink alcohol. But there was so much he didn't know about her. He knew every inch of her skin; he could picture every fleck in her grey-blue eyes and recall every contour of her beautiful full-lipped mouth. He knew what it felt like to be inside her body, but he couldn't get inside her head. He reflected back on their relationship and realised it had been mostly about the sex. They had fallen in lust, smoking-hot lust that had consumed both of them into its spellbinding vortex. And kissing her a few minutes ago had proved their lust for each other had not died. It had smouldered for two years like long, spreading tree roots underground, just waiting for a spark to reignite an inferno.

Jago looked around the pathetic bedsit for any signs of Mollie's private life, but there no were photos of her family and friends. He frowned and thought back to the wedding planner asking Mollie who she wanted to invite to the wedding. He hadn't thought much of it at the time, but now it seemed glaringly obvious that Mollie had had no intention of going through with the wedding. There were so many red flags he hadn't seen or had chosen not to see, which made him even more furious with himself. Had he been so blind with lust he couldn't see she had set him up right from the start? Mollie had said her parents were dead and that all her other relatives such as uncles and aunts and cousins were living abroad and couldn't make it to the wedding. He hadn't met a single one of her friends, although she had mentioned going out with them for coffee or yoga and Pilates classes. That in itself should have alerted him to something. Who didn't introduce their partner to their friends? And when the wedding planner had asked if Mollie wanted someone to walk her up the aisle and give her away as per tradition, Mollie had said she didn't believe in such outdated nonsense. She had kept insisting on a small wedding, but of course his grandmother was having none of that. If one of her playboy grandsons was finally going to settle down, Elsie had wanted all the bells and whistles of a big, white wedding. Jago still had the blasted wedding cake and Mollie's wedding dress. He had them in one of the spare rooms at his London house like he was a male version of Miss Havisham from Dickens's *Great Expectations*. He'd kept it to remind himself to never let his guard down again. To never be so blindsided by lust that he proposed marriage. To never feel so deeply for anyone that gave them the power to hurt him.

Before Jago met Mollie, he'd had no intention of settling down. He wasn't the eldest, so Jack had more pressure on him to marry and produce an heir than either he or Jonas had. But one date had turned into two, then three, then weeks had gone by and he'd found himself more and more in lust with Mollie. He couldn't get enough of her. He decided to ask her to marry him, not on a whim or impulsively. He'd thought about it for weeks before he decided it was the right thing to do. He'd wanted the commitment from her, the security of marriage that would guarantee she was his and his alone. Their connection was so like the passionate one of his parents. He had wanted to be with her all the time just as his parents had adored being in each other's company. Jago didn't believe himself to be in love, but sometimes he wondered if he had got scarily close to it. But he had been duped by Mollie right from the beginning. And yet when he kissed her earlier, he could not find it in himself to hate her for jilting him. Did that make him a lust-driven fool?

Jago ground his teeth, annoyed with himself for not putting the pieces together until now. Two years ago, he had been thinking with his hormones instead of his head. His lust for Mollie had blurred his judgement, opening him up to ridicule as a jilted groom when she bolted. He hated thinking about that day and all those that followed. Cynicism was in his blood, hardwired into his personality, and yet he had not seen the signs that were so obvious in hindsight.

But this time would be different. He was paying her to act the role of his fiancée. Yes, they might kiss and hold hands in front of his family, but he would take it no further.

But you still want her. Badly.

Jago dismissed the voice of his conscience. He wasn't going to allow his hormones to override his common sense. Not again.

CHAPTER FIVE

Mollie packed a few necessities in her weekend bag, but most of her clothes were not up to the standard of a Wilde gathering, especially for Jago's grandmother's birthday party. Mollie wore a uniform for work and casual clothes in her free time. She did not go out to dinner or on dates, and apart from the little black dress she was wearing, the only other glamorous outfit she possessed was one Jago had bought her two years ago. She located it in the back of her small wardrobe and took it out and held it up for inspection. It was still wrapped in drycleaner's plastic, but she knew it was the dress to wear. The baby-blue silk made her eyes pop and clung to her figure in all the right places. She took it off the hanger and rolled it up, plastic wrapping in place and packed it along with a pair of heels and a matching slimline evening purse.

A short time later, Mollie joined Jago in the combined kitchen and sitting room. He was pacing the floor with a frown on his face and turned to face her. 'Got what you need?'

'I think so.'

He strode over to take the bag for her. 'Let's go.'

A few minutes later, Jago led Mollie into his luxurious hotel suite. The difference from her bedsit was stark and reminded her of the different worlds they occupied. Jago was used to having the best of everything. He had never had to miss a meal in order to pay a bill. He not only had savings, but he also had investments—properties and share portfolios and who knew what else. All Mollie had was debt, despair and dread over what might happen to her brother if she didn't succeed in getting him the help he needed.

But this weekend was the solution to helping Eliot. She wouldn't have accepted a penny from Jago if it wasn't for her brother. Being with Jago in any context, real or pretend, was dangerous. Didn't their kiss prove it? Her mouth was still tingling from the passionate pressure of his. His kiss had awakened her ongoing desire for him, and as much as she wished she could turn it off, she knew it was impossible.

'Nice room,' Mollie said, sweeping her gaze around the suite, which was larger than any place she had ever lived in. She tried not to look at the king-size bed, but her gaze was drawn to it regardless. The snow-white sheets and artfully arranged pillows and the cashmere throw rug were of the highest quality. The soft lighting in the suite gave an intimate atmosphere to the space which was soothing, and the soft carpet under her feet threatened to swallow her up to the ankles. The stress and emotional roller-coaster events of the day suddenly caught up with Mollie, and she couldn't hold back a yawn.

'Time for bed?' Jago said.

Mollie gave the bed a sideways glance. 'Where are you going to sleep?'

He shrugged himself out of his jacket and hung it over the back of a chair. 'We've shared a bed before.'

Mollie swallowed a gulp but made sure her expression revealed nothing of her inner turmoil. 'Yes, but that was before, and this is now.'

One of his black brows rose in a sardonic arc. 'Don't you trust me to keep to my side of the bed?'

The problem was Mollie didn't trust herself. What if she reached for him during the night? What if she called out his name as she dreamed of him as she so often did? What if her body sensed him there and acted on instinct, moving to entwine her legs with his, to stroke his manhood to steel? She was getting hot and bothered just thinking about it.

Mollie affected a cool expression, but her lower body was already on fire. 'You told me you wouldn't lay a finger on me and yet you kissed me.'

'We kissed each other, Mollie.'

He was right. It had been entirely mutual, and it had actually been Mollie who had closed the gap between their mouths.

'You had every opportunity to tell me to back off, but you didn't,' Jago said. 'Why was that, hmm?'

Mollie wasn't sure she knew the answer to that, or at least none she wanted to share with him. Why had she allowed him to kiss her? And more to the point, why had she kissed him back so enthusiastically? Had her self-control vaporised the moment he strode back into her life?

She gave a careless shrug of her shoulders and placed her tote bag on the chair where he had hung his jacket. 'You always were a good kisser. I guess I wanted to see if you had got better or stayed the same.'

'And your assessment is…?'

Mollie gave him a flinty look. 'I don't think your robustly healthy ego needs any stroking from me.'

His eyes gleamed, and his mouth tilted in a smile that made her lower spine loosen. 'Do you want to have a shower before bed?'

She tried not to think of all the times they had showered together. Was he thinking of those sexy times too? The warm water cascading over their bodies, his erection thick and potent inside her, his deep thrusts and the clever caressing of his fingers tipping her over the edge time and time again. No one had ever made her feel the level of ecstasy that Jago Wilde had. No one had ever sent her senses into such a tailspin, leaving her body tingling for hours afterwards. Two years on and a frisson danced through her when she thought of him making love to her. It was one of the reasons she hadn't ventured back into dating. She wanted to hold those memories of him for as long as she could.

Mollie sent him a frosty look that was at total odds

to the fire burning in her lower body. 'Just in case you get any funny ideas, I'll be locking the door.'

'Good idea.' His smile was faintly mocking as if he knew how tempted she was to ask him to join her.

Mollie turned and rummaged in her bag for her evening skin products and the sleepwear she had brought. The two-piece pyjama set was hardly what one would describe as *sexy*, but it was comfortable and modest. Right now, modesty seemed the right way to go.

The bathroom was a glass-and-marble wonderland with brass taps and underfloor heating. There was a walk-in shower as well as a deep claw-foot bath and twin basins set in front of a large gilt-edged mirror. There were gloriously soft towels and luxury soaps and hair and beauty products to choose from. Mollie put her own things on the marble counter and then went back to the door and locked it. She stood stock-still for a moment, listening for any sound of Jago on the other side of the door, but she couldn't hear a thing.

After a relaxing shower, Mollie turban-wrapped her hair in a towel and then dressed in her cotton pyjamas. She did her evening skin care routine and then unwound the towel on her head to let her hair fall about her shoulders. There was a top-quality hair dryer in a drawer below the basins, so she gave her hair a quick blast to remove the excess moisture.

She looked at herself in the mirror and not for the first time wondered why Jago had been attracted to her. She saw herself as average, not stunning, but she had the advantage of being trained in beauty therapy, so she knew how to make the most of her assets. But without the professional mask of her make-up, she looked a lot younger and far more vulnerable than she wanted to. There was a haunted look in her eyes that she took great pains to hide when not alone. The constant worry of her brother's welfare wore her down to the point where she felt older than she was. In two years, she would be thirty, and for more than half her life she had tried to keep Eliot out of harm's way. What if she failed? What if, after every sacrifice and effort she had made, her brother didn't make it? Mollie knew the statistics on long-term drug and alcohol addiction. She could already see the negative effects on her younger brother's health. The chronic diseases that could only be managed, not cured. As hard as it was to be in Jago's company, she had to see this through for her brother's sake.

There was a light knock at the door. 'Are you finished in there?' Jago asked.

Mollie blinked away the ghosts in her eyes. 'Yep.' She took a deep breath and pushed herself away from the marble counter, hung up her used towels on the warming rail then went over to unlock the door.

Jago was no longer standing close to the bathroom door but was sitting on one of the plush velvet armchairs, scrolling through his phone. He glanced up as she came into the room, his eyes running over her dove-grey pyjamas. 'Feel better?'

'Much.'

He rose from the chair and slipped his phone in his trouser pocket. 'Go to bed. You look exhausted.'

Mollie shook out her still slightly damp hair. 'Yes, well, it's been quite a day.'

Jago came up close to her, his expression serious. 'I meant it when I said I don't expect you to sleep with me as part of the deal.'

Mollie swept the tip of her tongue over her lips, her gaze lowering to his mouth as if drawn by a powerful magnet. His mouth was set in a firm line, but she knew how quickly it could soften with one press of her lips to his. She brought her gaze back to his, her heart pounding unevenly in her chest. She fought with herself to remain strong, resolute in not caving in to her body's desire for him, but it still pulsed and throbbed in her blood regardless. 'If you think I would sleep with you for money, you are seriously mistaken.'

Jago's features tensed, and his gaze heated. 'Then, what was our past relationship all about, if not money?'

Mollie compressed her lips into a tight line, her spine ramrod stiff. 'I know someone as cynical as you won't believe it, but I did genuinely have feelings for you.'

'Love?' He said the word so mockingly she could feel a blush staining her cheeks. 'If that's how love acts, then I want no part of it.'

'I'm sorry I hurt you, but at the time I had no other choice.'

His expression was scathing. 'Your choice was to fill your bank account with money and make a fool of me in the process. But did you ever consider what your actions did to other members of my family? My grandmother, for instance?'

Back then, Mollie had had no time to think about anything but keeping those images out of circulation. It was only much later that she thought of Jago's grandmother, who was so excited about her middle grandson finally settling down. Elsie must have been so bitterly disappointed and sad for her grandson, falsely believing him to be in love with his runaway fiancée. Mollie had briefly thought of his brothers too, but she had only met them a handful of times, and while she knew they would abhor what she had done to Jago, she didn't think they would give her another thought. Out of sight, out of mind.

As for Maxwell Wilde...well, Mollie tried not to think about him at all. But even so, she often found herself wondering why it had been Maxwell who had been approached by the blackmailer and not Jago. As her fiancé, surely Jago should have been the target for blackmail? He had wealth equal to if not greater than that of his grandfather.

'I can only imagine how upset your grandmother must have been,' Mollie said then added with a note of bitterness, 'As for your grandfather, I'm sure he was glad to see the back of me. He never liked me. He never considered me good enough.'

'No one is ever good enough for my grandfather

including, at times, his wife and grandsons.' Jago's tone was as bitter as hers had been, his frown deep.

Mollie had always wondered what Jago's childhood had been like growing up with such an overbearing grandfather as his guardian. Jago was only five when his parents were killed. It was such a young age to lose his primary caregivers, but to be then raised by an impossible-to-please grandfather must have added another level of trauma.

'Was your father good enough for him?' It was bold of her to ask such a question when Mollie already knew he had refused to talk about his parents on every occasion she had raised the topic.

There was a beat or two of weighted silence.

Jago let out a rough-edged sigh and stepped away from her. 'Just go to bed, Mollie. I need to shower and shave.' He turned and entered the bathroom, closing the door with a click that was like a full stop. End of conversation.

Mollie released a long breath and glanced at the bed again. Jago expected her to share the bed with her, but he didn't want to share anything about his parents. They had died nearly thirty years ago, and yet Jago refused to tell her anything about what he had gone through in being bereaved at such a tender age. While she had her own reasons for not talking about her parents, Mollie longed for Jago to trust her enough to tell her about his. She had done some research of her own and found images of his parents online. His father had been a striking man with the

Wilde jet-black hair and chiselled jaw and deep-set blue eyes and aristocratic bearing. Jago's mother had been like a supermodel in looks: a gorgeous brunette with a wide smile, sparkling brown eyes and a willowy build. They had died in a small-plane crash on their way to a weekend away together. Several of the press articles had mentioned that tragic as the crash was, it was fortunate the three Wilde boys were not with their parents in the aircraft. One article had shown a photo of the boys standing outside the front of Wildewood Manor the month before they lost their parents. Jack, the eldest was standing beside Jago with a cheeky smile. Jago's smile had looked genuine enough, but Jonas, the youngest, had not been smiling at all, as if he saw the world through a more serious lens than his two older brothers.

Mollie sighed and brought herself back to the present by listening to the sound of Jago showering. She knew so much about his body, had explored every inch of it in detail, and yet he had not given her access to his past. It was a cordoned-off area, a do-not-go-there place she could only speculate about because of his point-blank refusal to speak of it.

Just like you.

Mollie knew it was hardly fair of her to badger Jago to reveal all about his childhood when she had told him nothing but lies about her own. But she hated talking about her childhood. It was something she wanted to erase from her memory, to keep the pain and distress out of her mind. Talking about it stirred up memories and flashbacks that gave her nightmares.

Mollie heard the shower stop, and she quickly dived into the bed and brought the covers up to her chin. She turned on her side, facing away from the bathroom, and closed her eyes, willing herself to sleep. But she was aware of every sound Jago made, and her body refused to relax enough to get anywhere near sleeping, even though she was tired from the events of the day. She curled up a bit more, adjusting the pillow under her head, breathing in the clean, fresh smell of the bed linen. Jago seemed to be taking an inordinately long time, so she tried some other relaxation techniques to get her body and her mind to relax, until finally she found herself sinking into the cloud of the mattress and the softness of the pillow, and her mile-a-minute brain slowed…slowed… and shut down…

Jago came out of the bathroom with a towel slung around his hips. Mollie's slim form was facing away from him, and she was curled up like a comma. Her breathing was slow and even, which meant she was asleep or doing an excellent job of pretending to be. He moved to the other side of the bed, glancing at her face to see if she responded to his presence, but her eyelids remained closed. He had to stop himself leaning down to press a kiss to her cheek and gently run his fingers through the fragrant silk of her hair. He had to stop himself thinking about all the times he had slipped in between the sheets with her and engaged in bed-wrecking sex. He had to find some way of resisting the magnetic pull of her. He could have saved himself this agony by booking separate rooms, but he didn't trust her enough not to disappear again.

Jago sighed and took off the towel and stepped into a pair of boxer shorts. He usually slept naked, but he decided a layer of fabric was called for to keep himself in check. He turned back to his side of the bed and got in, glancing at Mollie to see if she was aware of his presence, but she remained in the same relaxed position, her bee-stung mouth slightly parted as she slept. He turned on his side and watched her for endless minutes, fighting the urge to stroke his hand down the satinlike skin of her shoulder. He couldn't take his eyes off her mouth, remembering how soft and pliable it had felt beneath his. One kiss was never going to be enough, and yet he had to keep his distance to avoid being sucked into her sensual force field.

He clenched his hand into a fist and turned onto his back, his body throbbing with the raw need she triggered in him. He let out another sigh and turned to switch off the bedside table light, cloaking the suite in darkness. He lay there for what felt like hours, unable to sleep, unable to stop thinking about her lying within touching distance.

Mollie made a soft murmuring sound and moved closer, her eyes still shut in sleep. One of her legs brushed against his, and his blood surged to his groin.

This was your idea, buddy.

His conscience gave him a mocking prod. Yes, it had been Jago's idea to keep Mollie with him, not just to stop her running away again but to prove to himself he could resist her. But kissing her had stirred his blood to fever pitch, and he wanted her more than ever. No other lover turned him on the way Mollie did. She only had to look at him a certain way and he was hot and hard and ready. The chemistry between them was as electrifying as before, if not more so. He had promised himself he wouldn't act on it unless she wanted him to.

Jago closed his eyes, but he could still smell her, the shampoo she used, the lotions and potions combined with her own natural scent. It was like a drug to him. He wanted to breathe more of her in. Would there ever be a time when he didn't want her any more? He had spent the last two years thinking of her, dreaming of her, aching for her. It had to stop. Mollie was a fraud, a gold-digger who had royally screwed him over. He had to remember he had been completely taken in by her, and he couldn't let it happen again. He would have to have an even tighter rein on his emotions to make sure she didn't get under his guard like the last time. He hated thinking about that day before the wedding when he came back, excited about getting married the following day. Mollie hadn't responded to a single call or text, but he reassured himself she was preoccupied with wedding preparations. But then he'd arrived at Wildewood to find the place in an uproar. His grandfather had taken him aside to tell him Mollie had left.

'She's gone. She's bolted. She's not coming back. Get over it.'

He still remembered the sound of his grandfather's voice, the deep timbre of it reminiscent of when he had delivered the tragic news of Jago's parents' death.

'They've gone. They're not coming back. Get over it.'

Was that why Jago was having so much trouble getting over her? Moving on with his life? He had a problem with processing grief, but then, who wouldn't after losing their parents so young? Not that he talked about it, even with his brothers. His friends were as casual as his lovers. He didn't allow people to get close, which was why Mollie had been such an exception. He *felt* close to her even though he hadn't told her everything about his past. There was a meaningful connection with her, an invisible bond he had only ever felt with his parents. He had trouble believing she was a gold-digger, as his grandfather had insisted she was. He still had trouble believing it, but how could her behaviour be explained any other way? He wished now he had not let his pride prevent him from finding her and asking her what the hell had gone wrong. Why hadn't he stood up for her? A niggle of worry began to wind its way through his brain. If Mollie was the gold-digger his family believed her to be, why wasn't he accepting it? Why did one tiny flicker of hope burn in his chest that there was some other explanation for her actions? But she had sold his specially designed engagement ring. He had asked a jewellery expert to keep a look out for it, hoping he would be proved wrong, but it had turned up in a pawn shop, and he'd had to accept she had sold it. Could he forgive her for it? The disposal of his ring had felt like another savage jab to his heart.

Mollie shifted again in her sleep, her movements not so relaxed this time. She flung one of her arms out, almost clocking him on the chin. Her face screwed up like she was having some sort of nightmare. 'No, no, no,' she cried and began to thrash her limbs.

Jago gathered her closer, guiding her head to his chest, his hand gently stroking the back of her head to settle her. 'Shhh, Mollie. Relax, babe. I'm here.'

She moved against him with a soft whisper. 'Eliot?'

Jago stiffened like he had been snap-frozen. His gut tightened like someone was clenching his intestines in a brutal blood-blocking grip. His heart cramped like someone had punched him in the chest.

Who the freaking hell was Eliot?

He glanced down at Mollie draped across his chest, but her eyes were still closed, and her breathing rate had slowed down. Two years had passed since she'd jilted him. She could have had any number of lovers since him. Why was he feeling such strong emotions about it? He had nothing to be jealous about: he had slept with other people too. Not as many as the press had made out, but enough to try and erase Mollie from his muscle memory. Not that it had worked, but still. He had no right to judge her for moving on with her life, other than she had taken his grandfather's money to do it and then sold the ring Jago had designed for her. It suited him to allow Mollie to think she was wearing a replica of his ring when in fact it was the original she had sold. The irony of it amused him: she was pretending to be his fiancée, believing the engagement ring to be as fake as their current relationship. There was a risk she might sell the ring again if she realised it was genuine, but it was a risk he was prepared to take. Although it was an expensive ring by most people's standards, he had enough money to bear the loss.

The only thing that niggled at him was there was nothing fake about the desire he still felt for her, and that was a problem he had yet to solve. As were those indefinable feelings that lingered in his heart which he was not ready or willing to examine too closely.

CHAPTER SIX

MOLLIE WOKE EARLY to find herself alone in the bed. The space beside her was crumpled, as was the pillow, so she assumed Jago had spent some of the night with her, although not reaching for her as he had done so often in the past. She sat upright and pushed the tangle of her hair out of her eyes then found Jago seated in one of the velvet chairs in the suite, his forearms resting on his knees and his midnight blue gaze trained on her.

She noted the dark shadows beneath his eyes and his tousled hair, which if anything made him look even more broodingly attractive, like a Gothic hero from the classics. 'You look like you didn't sleep too well.'

Jago leaned back and dragged a hand down his face, the rasp of his morning stubble against his skin sounding overly loud in the silence. 'Turns out you're right.' He pushed himself out of the chair and came over to stand beside her side of the bed, still with his gaze locked on hers. 'Pleasant dreams?' His tone had a sour note to it that made the hairs on the back of her neck stand up like miniature soldiers.

Mollie frowned at him, not sure how to handle him in this mood. 'Stop towering over me and looking at me like that. It's not my fault you didn't sleep well.'

'I beg to differ.'

'You were the one who insisted on us sharing a room,' she pointed out.

There was a pulsing beat of silence.

'Who is Eliot?'

Mollie stiffened, her gaze wary as it held his penetrating one. She took a steadying breath and fashioned her features into a cool mask. 'None of your damn business, that's who.'

His expression tightened, and his mouth went into a flat line. 'Have there been many lovers since you called off our wedding? Or was this Eliot guy in the picture before we got together?'

Mollie tossed the bed covers aside and got out of bed, furious with him for thinking she might have had a lover on the side while engaged to him. But how else could she explain without telling him about her brother? 'How many lovers have you had?' she shot back with a scalding look.

'Five.'

'Only five?' She coughed up a laugh that had not an ounce of humour in it. 'You surprise me. I thought it would be closer to fifty.'

Something glittered in his eyes that reminded her of unreachable stars in the night sky. 'I seem to recall I told you when we first met, you shouldn't take as gospel everything that is reported about me or my brothers in the press.'

Mollie was still trying to contain her shock at his number of lovers. Only five? Even if the press got it wrong occasionally, she knew enough about his strong sex drive to find such a low number of lovers surprising. Jago Wilde was a man in the prime of his life, full-blooded and virile and rich and handsome beyond belief. Why hadn't he gone back to his profligate playboy ways? He would have had numerous opportunities to do so over the last two years; women swarmed around him like bees to exotic pollen.

'You still haven't answered my question,' Jago said. 'Who is Eliot?'

Mollie compressed her lips, torn between wanting to keep her private life private but feeling a strange need to share her burden with someone. Someone who would understand and not judge her for her hardscrabble origins and the damage that had been caused to her and her brother as a result. Was Jago that person? But how could someone from such a wealthy and privileged background ever understand what she and her brother had gone through? But then, she wondered if by sharing a little of her background, Jago might lower his guard and talk about the loss of his parents. She decided to take a chance. 'Eliot is my brother, my half-brother really. We don't share the same father.'

Jago's frown deepened. 'I thought you said you were an only child?'

Mollie folded her arms across her body. 'I'm not. I may well have other half-siblings for all I know. I've never met my biological father. Eliot and I share a mother.'

'You told me you were an orphan. So that was a lie too?' Jago was standing with his hands on his hips, looking down at her with a glimmer of hurt in his gaze that made her heart contract.

'I don't know if my biological father is alive or not, but I know for sure my mother is dead.' Mollie decided against telling him the rest of that ghastly story. Revisiting that time in her life was too traumatising.

Jago turned away from her and paced the floor like he was trying to maintain control of himself. He finally turned to face her once more, his expression still cast in lines of confusion, hurt and anger all mixed together. 'Why did you lie to me?'

Mollie gave a dismissive shrug of her shoulders. 'I try to distance myself from my upbringing. The only way I could find to do it successfully was to pretend it hadn't happened. I made up a backstory for myself that was easier to live with.'

Jago's frown was so severe his brows met over his eyes. 'But I was your fiancé, Mollie. Surely, I deserved to know the truth about the woman I intended to marry.'

Mollie reached for a hotel bathrobe and wrapped herself in it like she was putting on a coat of armour. She turned to face Jago again, her expression cool. 'Why were you intending to marry me? You never told me you loved me. Surely that is Marriage Proposal Protocol 101?'

Jago deftly avoided answering her question by throwing one back at her. 'Was that a lie when you told me you loved me?'

Mollie absently twirled the engagement ring on her left hand. 'I did love you, Jago.'

'You said that in the past tense.' Jago said without any trace of emotion in his voice as if he was simply making an observation, one that meant little or nothing to him. But then, why would it mean anything to him? He hadn't loved her. He hadn't said the words she'd most wanted to hear. He had proposed marriage without saying he loved her. She should never have accepted, except she had foolishly believed he would change, that he would open his heart to her. How many women made the same mistake? Too many. But she had felt wanted for the first time in her life, and it had made it impossible to say *no* to him. He had made her feel safe, secure and wanted, and it had been enough for her back then.

'That was two years ago,' Mollie said, folding her arms to stop herself playing with the ring. 'A lot of things have happened since then.'

His handsome features were now cast in guarded lines. 'So tell me about your half-brother.'

Mollie sighed and sat on the edge of the bed, her hands clasped in her lap. 'Eliot has…issues.' She began to scratch at the inside of her wrist but then stopped and glanced up at Jago who was watching her intently. 'I've been responsible for his welfare for a long time. He's three years younger than me.' She looked down at her hands again, the fake engagement ring glinting at her like an accusing eye.

You failed him. You allowed Eliot's life to be destroyed. You don't deserve to be happy.

Her inner critic was relentless in its disparagement of her failings where Eliot was concerned.

'Why did you take it upon yourself to be responsible for him?' Jago asked, still frowning darkly.

Mollie stood from the bed in one jerky movement. 'Because none of the adults in our life were up to the task.'

Concern was written large on Jago's face. 'Who took care of you?' There was a hollow-sounding quality to his voice she had never heard in it before, as if he was picturing her as a young child trying her best to survive.

'I took care of both of us,' Mollie said. Her earliest memories were not of being cuddled or nurtured by her mother but of abuse and neglect, the gnawing pain of hunger and the cold-footed fear that tiptoed up and down her small spine on a daily basis. 'My mother and her partner were drug addicts who had no idea how to look after little kids. We were in and out of foster care, but every time we were sent back to my mother, who had supposedly cleaned up her act, it would all begin again. The drinking, the drugs, the parties, the creepy boyfriend who had brutal methods for controlling little kids who were crying with hunger.'

Jago swallowed deeply, the sound audible in the silence. 'Mollie...' There was an anguished quality to his voice and his eyes looked pained. 'Did he...hurt you?' His hands were clenched into tight fists as if he wanted to track down her mother's criminal boyfriend and deal with him then and there.

'I taught myself to go somewhere else in my head when he hit me. But Eliot was so little, and he didn't stop crying, so my mother's boyfriend used to slip him a pill to make him sleep. I think that's why Eliot has such addiction problems now, that and the abuse he suffered in foster care, which I blame myself for.'

The shock and horror on Jago's face was painful to witness. 'Why do you blame yourself?'

'Because I should have done a better job of protecting him. He was only three.'

'But you were a child, only six years old yourself. The foster carers were supposed to be protecting you both.'

'That's not how it always works, although to be fair, there are some wonderful foster carers out there. We were mostly placed in care together, but occasionally we were separated. One of the times we were apart, I begged to be with him, and finally we were sent to another foster home. On the surface it looked like a wonderful family to be in. The foster parents were nice people, but there was an occasional visitor to the house, the brother of the foster father. He...'

Mollie swallowed tightly, barely able to get the words out. 'He... Well, without going into too much detail, my little brother became a victim of his...attentions. Eliot didn't tell me about it until he was an adult. I felt so guilty because I thought the uncle was charming. I would never have left Eliot alone with him if I'd realised.' Mollie knew deep down she wasn't really to blame for her brother's abuse—it was the perpetrator who was responsible and should be shouldering the blame—but her sense of failure haunted her regardless.

Jago came over to her and took her hands in his. Concern shone in his eyes. 'You must stop blaming yourself. Men like that groom not just their victim but the whole family, even whole communities.'

'I can never forgive myself,' Mollie said. 'Eliot is a train wreck but I can't give up on him. He's been in and out of rehab, but he doesn't stay long enough for it to take any effect.'

Jago put his arms around her and drew her close in a hug. Mollie leaned into his solid warmth and let out a heavy sigh. He stroked her back in a soothing fashion, and her tight muscles slowly unclenched until she melted against him. This was why she'd fallen in love with him in the first place. He'd made her feel safe for the first time in her life. She was a little bobbing boat in a wildly unpredictable ocean, and he was a lighthouse, a safe harbour, an anchor to hold her steady.

'Where is Eliot now?' Jago's voice rumbled against her left ear.

'In a very expensive rehabilitation clinic in Glasgow. He's been there six months, but he needs to stay for a whole year for it to be effective.'

There was a silence that Mollie measured with the slow steady thump-thump-thump of Jago's heartbeat next to her ear.

After a long moment, he held her a little apart from him so he could look down at her. His expression was contorted with so many emotions, they flickered through his gaze as if he was thinking back over their relationship and their break-up and putting things together in his mind. 'You took the money my grandfather offered you to help your brother.' It was a statement, not a question, as if he had come to a final conclusion about her actions.

Mollie grimaced. 'I'm sorry I can't tell you anything...'

'Because of the NDA?'

She gave a tiny nod, her lips pressed together before she spilled any more of the horrid secrets she carried. Heavy and burdensome secrets that had weighed her down for so long.

Jago picked up her hands again and gave them a gentle squeeze. 'Why didn't you come to me for help? I could have paid for Eliot's rehab.' There was a gruff edge to his voice, a side note of hurt that she hadn't considered him as her go-to person.

Mollie was tempted to tell him about the deepfakes, but she couldn't risk it, not until she saw Maxwell Wilde's reaction to her being back in Jago's life, albeit temporarily. She pulled her hands out of Jago's with a strained smile. 'Hindsight is a beautiful thing, is it not? There are so many things I would do differently if I could.'

Jago was looking at her as if he were seeing her for the first time. The real her, not the made-up version. It made her feel exposed and vulnerable, and yet there was a part of her that was relieved she had told him about her brother. She felt like she was no longer carrying that emotional burden on her own.

'Mollie...' Jago scraped his hair back with his hand then dropped it back down to his side. 'I think we need to get to Wildewood Manor as soon as possible. You need to call your boss and tell her you're not coming in. In fact, tell her you're not coming back.'

Mollie stared at him, not sure whether to be annoyed at his taking command of her employment situation or relieved he was rescuing her from a job she had grown to loathe. The clients she loved; it was her boss that was the problem. 'But—'

'I'll cover any expenses you have until you find another job.'

'You're making me sound like a kept woman or, even worse, a gold-digger.'

Jago twisted his mouth in a rueful manner. 'I can see you're not going to forgive me for that, are you? I can't forgive myself for ever believing it.'

'I'm not a vengeful person, Jago.'

He came back over to her and lifted her chin with the tip of his index finger, locking her gaze with his.

His eyes were so dark a blue they reminded her of a bottomless ocean. An ocean she wanted to dive into and explore those hidden depths. His eyes lowered to her mouth, lingering there for so long she could feel her lips tingling in anticipation of the descent of his mouth.

'If I kiss you,' he said, 'it will delay our departure.'

'How long a kiss are you thinking?' Mollie's voice was just a whisper of sound, liberally laced with longing.

He lifted both hands up to frame her face, his eyes holding hers. 'Longer than I anticipated when I first approached you about this weekend.' His thumbs moved like twin metronomes, slowly stroking her cheeks in a tender but blood-heating manner.

Mollie was finding it hard to remember to breathe. Her heart was beating with hammer blows that threatened to shatter her rib cage. Her feminine core was stirring in response to the tempting closeness of his body. She could feel the thickening of his erection pressed against her. 'They're your rules. You can break them if you want.'

The dark intensity of his eyes sent a wave of heat through her flesh. Molten heat that left spot fires in its wake. 'Not unless you want me to break them.'

Break them. Break them. Break them.

Her blood was pounding with the chanting of her feverish need. Mollie brought her mouth closer to his until there was barely space for a puff of air. 'I want you to break them.'

Jago's mouth fused to hers in a slow and deliberate kiss that sent shock waves of delight through her body. Tingles raced up and down her spine, fireworks went off in her blood. Her body melted with the hot, moist dew of desire triggered by his tongue entering her mouth and mating with hers. Her hands wound up around his neck, her fingers delving into his hair, stroking and tugging in the way she knew he liked. He groaned against her mouth and brought her closer to the hard ridge of his erection.

'I want you so bad.'

'I want you too.'

He eased back to look at her. 'Are you sure?'

'It's only for this weekend, right?'

Something flickered in his gaze like an interruption in the transmission of a film. 'It will certainly add authenticity to our game of pretend,' he said, glancing back at her mouth as if he couldn't keep his eyes off it.

Mollie raised herself up on tiptoes, bringing her body closer to his. 'I thought you were in a rush to get to Wildewood Manor?'

He grinned at her and planted his hands on her hips, tugging her even closer. 'I have a private jet on standby. The pilot will wait until I see to some outstanding business.'

Mollie raised her brows. 'Is that how you see me?'

His mouth came down to just above hers. 'You are more along the lines of unfinished business,' he said and sealed her mouth with his.

CHAPTER SEVEN

TOUCHING MOLLIE AGAIN stirred every cell in Jago's body into throbbing excitement. He ached for her with a bone-deep need that had pulsed in his flesh for two long years. His mouth devoured hers like he was unable to get enough of its sweet taste, one he had not forgotten. Her mouth was soft and pliable beneath his, her murmurs of encouragement making him as hard as stone. His hands were on her hips, holding her to his pounding need, relishing in the feel of her so close. He entered her mouth on a deep sigh of pleasure—or was it relief? He could barely get his thoughts in any sort of order. All he wanted was to lose himself in the nectar of her mouth, to feel her tongue dancing and duelling with his.

Mollie wound her arms around his neck and began to play with the ends of his hair, and a wave of electrifying pleasure flowed through him. Her touch was magic to him; he had never forgotten the way she could turn him on with a simple look or touch.

Jago deepened the kiss, groaning against her pillow-soft lips, wanting all of her. His hands moved up to gently shape her breasts, and she murmured her approval against his lips.

He eased back to look down at her. 'I want to touch you all over.'

He lowered his mouth back to hers in a lingering kiss, his hands sliding under her pyjama top, his senses going wild as he touched the gentle slopes of her breasts. Her nipples were tight buds, and he took his mouth from hers to take each in his mouth, licking, tasting, teasing her flesh into even tighter points.

Mollie's hands tugged at his trouser fastening, and his heart raced with excitement. He loved how enthusiastic she was about making love with him. In record time they were both naked, and he drank in the sight of her body, his blood pounding through his body with anticipation.

He ran his hands over her from her shoulders to her hips, tugging her closer so she could feel his need against her belly. 'You drive me to distraction. I want you like I want no one else.'

Mollie reached between their bodies and stroked his length, and he groaned in delight. He slipped his hand down to her most female of flesh, and within seconds she was falling apart, gasping and arching her spine as she orgasmed. When it was finally over, she looked at him in a dazed manner, her eyes wide, her mouth open, her breathing ragged.

'Good?' Jago asked with a smile.

'Fast and furious and fabulous,' Mollie said, her cheeks a soft rose-petal pink.

How could he not feel a measure of pride in being able to pleasure her so quickly? Her responsiveness to him was so delightful, and it heightened his pleasure. 'I need to get a condom.' He let her go just long enough to grab a condom from his wallet, applying it with haste as his need for her hummed and throbbed in his blood.

Jago took her by the hand and led her to the bed, coming down on top of her with a sigh of pure bliss. It was like coming home after a long journey. Her arms went around him, her legs opening to welcome him. He entered her with a guttural groan that sounded almost primal, the silky tightness of her wrapping around him, sending him wild. But his need for her was primal: it had driven him crazy for the last two years. He had missed her so damn much—the taste of her, the feel of her in his arms, the spine-tingling chemistry they had together. He began to thrust, slowly at first, allowing her time to get used to him again, but Mollie arched her spine and bucked her hips, making whimpering noises, urging him to speed up. He drove harder and faster, losing himself in the tight grip of her body, his senses reeling as his need for release built like a rising tide. He slipped one of his hands between their rocking bodies, teasing the swollen wet nub of her clitoris until she fell apart again. He let himself go with her, her body's contractions around him intensifying his enjoyment. Every muscle in his body tensed, then he finally exploded, spilling his essence…and then a wave of peace and calm flowed through his entire body, leaving him spent and relaxed against her.

Jago couldn't move. Didn't want to move. He was enjoying the feel of Mollie's arms around him, her soft hands stroking the small of his back and then sliding over his buttocks. It was like she was rediscovering his contours, her hands shaping him as he had shaped her. If only they could stay in this intimate bubble, where no one else could intrude. But he had to get to the manor and deal with whatever reaction his grandfather would have to him bringing home his runaway fiancée.

Jago was still putting together the complicated pieces of the puzzle that was Mollie. Her need to protect and provide for her half-brother had been the focus of her life since childhood. How had he not found out about her background before now? The truth, not what she had chosen to tell him. Mollie had locked him out of her real-life circumstances, and yet she had claimed to love him.

But you've told her nothing about your childhood.

Jago's conscience reminded him of how many times he had locked her out of any discussion about his own history. Wasn't it time to let her know a little bit of what it had been like to lose his parents? But he hated being vulnerable. Maybe he was more like his grandfather than he wanted to admit, but he had always been taught that being vulnerable was a weakness. His grandfather had drummed it into Jago and his brothers: it would give people a tool to exploit you if you showed them your feelings. So Jago had locked his away and denied or ignored them.

Jago finally eased his weight onto his elbows to look at Mollie. 'Am I too heavy for you?'

Mollie looked up at him as if she couldn't believe he was real. Her hand came up and stroked his jaw just as she used to do in the past. 'No.' She gave a soft sigh and looked at his mouth, then traced around it with her index finger, making his lips tingle and a hot shiver shimmy down his spine.

Jago brushed a strand of her hair back from her face. Then he captured one of her hands and brought it up to his lips, pressing a soft kiss to her fingertips, his eyes holding hers. 'Forgive me for thinking you were a gold-digger. I'm annoyed at myself for insulting you like that, when all the time you were trying to take care of your brother.'

A flicker of pain went through her gaze, and her mouth twisted in a rueful fashion. 'I should have told you the truth before, but I hate talking about my childhood. It's retraumatising.'

'I get it,' Jago said, stroking his finger down the ski slope of her nose. 'I hate talking about mine too.'

Her eyes moved back and forth between each of his like she was searching for the real him. Like she could see right into his soul. Like she could see every painful feeling he had locked away inside himself.

'Do you ever talk to your brothers about your parents?' Her voice was soft, tiptoe soft as if she knew she was treading on territory that was intensely painful for him.

Jago laced his fingers with hers. 'Rarely, if ever. Our grandfather forbade us as children to talk about them. He thought it would make us stronger if we just accepted that they were gone and moved on with our lives.'

'So you weren't allowed to grieve?'

'Nope.'

'Did you go to the funeral?'

'Only Jack and I went. Jonas was considered too young at only three. But once the wake was over, we were forbidden to talk about our parents to each other, our grandmother or anyone.'

'Not even to your grandmother?' Shock rippled through her tone.

'My grandfather told us it would upset her too much, but looking back now, I think she would have benefited from talking about them. She, like us, was unable to grieve the way she needed to. She had a mental breakdown a couple of years later. She didn't leave the house for months.'

'Your grandfather has lot to answer for.' There was a hard edge to Mollie's voice, and a frown pulled at her forehead.

'He's got his faults, certainly, but I suspect he was so grief-stricken himself, allowing us to talk about our parents would have made it harder for him to carry on,' Jago said. 'He had to suddenly raise his grandchildren, comfort his wife and take over my father's business as well as his own.'

'You're very forgiving. What you've described is emotional abuse.'

Jago grimaced at the uncomfortable truth of her observation. 'I know, but it was a different time back then, and now that I've been overseeing his business affairs, I realise he was under an enormous amount of pressure.' He moved away so he could dispose of the condom, then standing beside the bed, held out a hand to her. 'We need to get a move on.'

Mollie put her hand in his, and he pulled her to her feet. Jago couldn't resist wrapping his arms around her and holding her close. He breathed in the scent of her hair, the fragrance of her skin, his lower body thickening all over again. Would he ever stop wanting her? His body still tingled from making love with her, his blood running feverishly hot as her pert breasts pushed against his chest.

'Jago?'

He gently stroked the back of her head. 'Mm?'

Mollie leaned back to look up at him, longing shining in her eyes. 'Do we have time for one more kiss?'

Jago smiled and brought her even closer to the pounding need of his body. 'Just the one.' And he lowered his head and covered her mouth with his.

An hour or so later, Mollie was sitting beside Jago on his private jet flying down to London. Her body was still tingling from his lovemaking, her heart rejoicing that he had finally talked a little about his childhood. It was like a nailed-up door had been opened a fraction between them, bringing them a little bit closer, not just physically but emotionally. She hadn't told him much more about her past, but being able to share about her worries over her brother was an enormous relief. It was so reassuring that Jago didn't believe she was responsible for her brother's issues. She had known it intellectually, but emotionally she had found it hard not to blame herself. But Mollie was uncomfortably aware of her other dark secret and couldn't imagine telling Jago the real reason she had taken his grandfather's payout and left. For now, it was easier to let Jago think it was all about helping to get Eliot into long-term rehab.

Jago was sitting beside her and reached for her hand, his dark blue gaze searching as it meshed with hers. 'There's something I'd like to understand a bit better. Why did my grandfather offer you money? Did you ask him for help?'

Mollie couldn't hold his gaze and instead looked at their joined hands. The fake engagement ring on her left hand glittered from the sunlight slanting in from the jet's window. 'I can't talk about it, Jago.'

'Can't or won't?'

She pressed her lips together for a moment before responding. 'Your grandfather is a very powerful man.'

'He can't do anything to hurt you, Mollie. I won't let him.' He squeezed her hand in a gesture of reassurance.

Mollie gave a scornful laugh. 'I told you before. He didn't think I was worthy of you. And given the circumstances of my childhood, he was probably right.'

Jago frowned. 'Look, he might be a grumpy old bigot, but it was my decision who to marry, not his. I still can't understand why you didn't tell me you needed money.'

'You were in New York signing off on that big property deal,' Mollie said. 'Your grandfather…found out I wasn't who I said I was, and—'

'What do you mean?' His voice had a sharp edge to it, his gaze piercing.

Mollie let out a stuttering sigh. 'My real name is Margaret Green. I changed my name when I turned eighteen. He must have done some sort of background check on me, and suffice it to say, my criminal past was anathema to him.' She figured sticking to some of the truth was better than telling Jago the whole truth. He had asked her to marry him without really knowing who she was.

Jago's frown was so deep it made him look intimidating. 'What crime did you commit?'

'Shoplifting.'

'How old were you?'

'Fifteen.'

'Wouldn't that have gone through the juvenile justice system? You don't usually get a conviction recorded when you're under eighteen unless it's for a more serious crime.'

'I know, but apparently your grandfather has contacts everywhere and uncovered my dirty little secret,' Mollie said. 'Wouldn't the press have loved to run that story? *Jago Wilde's Fiancée Was a Teenage Shoplifter.* Think of the shame I would have brought on your family.'

Jago's features were set in tense lines. 'So you took the money and ran.'

'It was for the best, Jago. Surely you see that now?' Mollie said, pulling her hand out of his. 'You weren't in love with me. We came from such different worlds. Do you really think we would have lasted the distance? We might well have been divorced or at least separated by now if we had married.'

His jaw worked for a moment, and his eyes glittered darkly. 'Are there any other things I should know about you?'

Mollie could feel heat pooling in her cheeks and had to look away to stare at the fluffy clouds outside the private jet. 'Everyone has things they don't want others to know about, even someone as perfect as you.'

Jago made a scoffing noise. 'I'm the last person to consider myself faultless. But I would appreciate it if you'd be honest and open with me. I don't want any more nasty surprises.'

Mollie's spine chilled to the marrow. What nastier surprise could there be than the one she was desperately hoping would stay secret? 'Will the press be at your grandmother's party?' she asked after a moment.

'No, we're keeping things quiet for Gran's sake.

She isn't supposed to have too much stimulation while she recovers from the concussion. There will only be handful of family and close friends.'

Mollie let out a sigh of relief. It would be hard enough facing Maxwell Wilde and Jago's older brother Jack, let alone the press. 'I guess she'd be even more confused if the press made a big deal about us being together again, especially when she thinks we never parted in the first place.'

Jago took Mollie's hand again and began to absently stroke the back of it with his thumb. His touch sent a wave of heat through her body, making her wonder how she was going to face the rest of her life without it. Her role as his fake fiancée was for the weekend and the weekend only.

'I've thought about that too, but I want her to have this weekend surrounded by those who love her. If there's a press leak, then I'll deal with it.' Jago gave her hand a reassuring squeeze.

Mollie did her best to smile at him, but her worries about the upcoming weekend were like tiny mice nibbling at the wainscoting of her mind. Returning to Wildewood Manor as Jago's fiancée was fraught with danger, but she couldn't back out now. On the way to the airport, she had briefly spoken to Eliot and his clinic doctor and been reassured Eliot was making slow but steady progress. Mollie had also informed her boss she wouldn't be returning to work. The money Jago had given her would tide her over for months, but she really wanted to open her own beauty clinic concentrating on skin care. Being her own boss was her goal. She wanted the security of knowing she was in control of her career, not at the mercy of someone else.

It wasn't long before they were off the plane and driving down to Wildewood Manor in the Cotswolds. As they got closer, Mollie's nerves became more agitated. The scenery was as picturesque as ever in early spring—bright egg-yolk daffodils everywhere, fresh green leaves unfurling on the trees, lush pastures, and even though there were light showers of rain, by the time Jago pulled into the grounds of the estate, the sun broke through and cast the manor in a golden light.

The imposing Elizabethan mansion was softened by its verdant surroundings. The garden leading to the front entrance was set along formal lines, with neatly trimmed yew hedges of different heights and shapes on either side of the flat, soft lawns that divided the wide stone pathway leading to the front door of the four-storey structure.

Jago drove around to the back where the family usually entered the building. He parked the car on the gravelled area that overlooked the rear gardens with a central fountain. There was a kitchen garden as well as a cottage-style one and, farther afield, a wild garden and a meadow beyond that leading to a lake and a densely wooded area in the distance.

Jago came around to open Mollie's door before she had undone her seatbelt, so engrossed was she in looking at Jago's childhood home again. It was undisputedly a beautiful property, but she wondered if all those rooms and gardens and meadows and woods had provided a cosy and nurturing environment for three grieving young children. Was there any amount of wealth and privilege that could compensate for such a heartbreaking loss?

Mollie unclipped her belt with a hand that wasn't as steady as she would have liked. She stepped out of the car, and Jago closed the door for her then held his hand out to her.

'Ready?' He was still wearing his sunglasses so she couldn't read his expression apart from the tight smile on his lips.

Mollie slipped her hand into his, her stomach tilting when his strong fingers wrapped around hers. 'I think so.' She took a deep breath and walked with him to the back door.

CHAPTER EIGHT

MOLLIE STEPPED OVER the threshold, still holding Jago's hand, her heart thumping like she had run all the way from London. One of the many servants who worked at Wildewood Manor greeted her with a welcoming smile. Obviously, Jago had briefed the staff beforehand about his plan to pretend they were still engaged.

'Welcome, Miss Mollie,' Harriet said. 'So lovely to see you again. Lady Wilde will be so pleased to see you.' She turned and addressed Jago. 'I've told young Jim to take your bags to your room. I'll serve afternoon tea in the Green Room in half an hour.'

'Thank you, Harriet,' Jago said. 'We'll freshen up and then go up and see Gran. Has there been any change?'

Harriet shook her head, her expression sombre. 'She sleeps a lot and is still confused.'

'And my grandfather?'

'He's in the study. Would you like me to get one of the maids to inform him you're here?' she offered.

'That won't be necessary,' Jago said in a wry tone. 'I'm sure he already knows.'

A short time later, Jago led Mollie to the room they had once shared on their occasional visits to Wildewood. Mollie stepped inside the commodious room, a host of memories assailing her. Not much had changed in the two years since she had jilted Jago. The decor was much the same, making her feel like she was stepping back in time. She went over to the windows to look at the stunning view outside. A shower of rain had recently fallen, and a rainbow stretched from one side of the wildflower-dotted meadow to the other.

Jago came up behind her and placed his hands on her shoulders. She could not stop herself from leaning back against him, relishing in the feel of his hard toned body against hers. Feeling that sense of safety she had never felt with anyone else. He turned her in his arms and looked down at her with a serious expression.

'I know I'm asking a lot of you to do this.'

'You're paying me a lot to do this,' Mollie reminded him.

His eyes moved back and forth between hers then dipped to her mouth. As if in slow motion, his head came down, and his lips briefly brushed hers. He pulled back but then gave a low, deep groan and lowered his mouth to hers again, kissing her lingeringly, deeply, passionately. Mollie wound her arms around his neck, standing on tiptoe so her hungry body could press against the tempting hardness of his. He groaned again then ran his hands down the sides of her body, cupping her bottom, holding her to his swollen length.

'I shouldn't be doing this,' Jago said against her mouth.

'Why not? We're engaged, aren't we?'

He framed her face in his hands, looking at her intently. 'I don't think I've ever wanted anyone as much as I want you.'

'I want you too.' More than she should given the circumstances. This game of pretend had some elements to it that were starting to feel frighteningly real. Her feelings, for instance. They had never disappeared but lain deep inside her like a dormant plant in winter. But spring had arrived, and the tiny buds of her feelings for Jago were popping up each time he kissed her. Every stroke of his hand, every incidental touch poured rich fertiliser on her feelings for him. The longer she spent with him, the stronger her love became. Why had she let him reawaken the fire? One kiss had blown her willpower to smithereens, and the irony was she had been the one who had allowed it. How could she stop this from getting any more serious? He had not known the real her when he'd asked her to marry him, but he was getting to know her now. He was closer to her than she had allowed anyone, and yet this was for this weekend only. How could she protect herself from further heartbreak? Or was the pleasure of his touch worth it? Silly question. Of course it was worth it. To feel wanted and desired, to feel alive in a way she hadn't for two long years.

Jago brought his mouth back down to hers in a kiss that was hot, sweet, sexy and tender at the same time. His hands gently skimmed over her, exploring her in exquisite detail, ramping up her desire like a match to dry tinder. He peeled away her top as she worked on the buttons of his shirt, desperate to be skin-on-skin with him. Jago kissed his way down from the soft skin of her neck, taking his time to reach her breasts. He savoured each one with his lips and tongue, stirring her senses into overload. His thumbs brushed over each of her nipples and the sensitive area around them, his touch making her gasp with longing. He lowered his mouth to her puckered flesh and subjected her to the most delicious sensual attention. Every hair on her head tingled at the roots, and the nerves beneath her skin went into a frenzy of excitement, her blood thrumming, humming with the pulse of her desire.

Mollie ran her hands over his muscled chest, delighting in the lean, hard contours of his gym-toned body. He hadn't followed the trend of waxing off his chest hair, and she ran her fingers through the springy dark whorls, and then pressed her naked breasts against his chest, enjoying the sensation of his hair tickling her soft skin.

Jago covered her mouth in another deep and hungry kiss, his hands holding her by the hips to keep her against the throb of his body. Mollie went for the waistband of his trousers then pulled down his zip to shape him through his underwear. He groaned against her lips, then worked on the rest of her clothes until they were both naked.

Jago kissed his way down her body, going down on bended knee in front of her, lavishing attention on the most intimate part of her body. Mollie had never allowed any other lover—not that she had had many—to perform such an intimate act on her before. It hadn't felt right, she hadn't felt comfortable, but with Jago it was as natural as breathing...except while he was doing it, breathing was almost impossible. Her heart raced, her pulse pounded as he separated her feminine folds with his lips and tongue. He knew exactly how to pleasure her, and pleasure her he did. Spectacularly. Earth-shatteringly. The powerful sensations took her by surprise, every nerve pulling tight before exploding in a cascade of sparks that rippled through her body in pulsating waves.

Jago moved back up her body, kissing her bellybutton, then her rib cage, her breasts and finally her mouth. He walked her backwards with his mouth still fused to hers, his hands guiding her by the hips until they landed together in a tangle of limbs on the king-size bed. He lifted his mouth from hers, looking down at her with lust-glazed eyes.

'Time to get a condom.' He sprang back off the bed and rummaged through his wallet for one.

'How many do you have in there?'

He sent her a devilish smile. 'Not enough. I'm going to have to grab some of Jack's.'

Mollie couldn't hold back a slight frown. 'You're okay with him knowing we're sleeping together this weekend?'

Jago paused in the process of unwrapping the condom he'd found. Nothing showed on his face, but she got the sense he was mulling over something in his mind. 'The only thing Jack will be concerned about is making sure Gran has a happy birthday. What you and I get up to while we're alone is our business, not his.'

'Are you close to him and Jonas?'

Jago came back to her on the bed, lying beside her, one of his hands resting on her belly, his eyes meshing with hers. 'Not as close as we might have been if our parents hadn't died.' A shadow drifted through his gaze just like the grey-tinged clouds scudding across the sky outside.

Mollie put a hand to his chiselled jaw and gently stroked it. 'I would imagine you'd be super close after experiencing such a tragic loss.'

His mouth twisted into a grimace. 'My grandfather sent us to different boarding schools so we couldn't rely on each other. It was supposed to be character-building for us.'

'That's cruel. You were so young to be left to cope on your own.'

'My grandmother was against it, but she had no say in the matter,' Jago said. 'She's of the era when women vowed to obey their husbands when they got married. I don't think I've ever seen her stand up for herself. She doesn't know how to.'

'Is it a happy marriage?'

Jago made a cynical sound at the back of his throat. 'Is any marriage happy all the time?' He blew out a long breath and continued. 'I suspect Gran realised early on that divorcing my grandfather would be an ugly battle, one she would lose in the end. She's remained faithful to him, but I don't think he's been faithful to her.'

Mollie's heart ached for his grandmother. To have spent so many years with a man who wasn't loyal to her must have chipped away at her self-confidence. 'You sound like you don't respect him much.'

'I don't. But he's too old to change now.'

Mollie chewed at her lower lip. 'I'm nervous about seeing him.'

Jago took his hand off her belly and trailed his splayed fingers through her hair, sending tingles up and down her spine. 'You don't need to be frightened of him. He can't hurt you, not while I'm around.'

He can hurt me more than you realise.

The words were on the tip of her tongue but she couldn't say them. She forced her mouth into an effigy of a smile, but inside she was quaking with fear. Fear of exposure, fear of some sort of payback from Maxwell Wilde for not abiding by the non-disclosure agreement he had insisted she sign. But she comforted herself with the knowledge that she had at least told Jago her primary reason for taking the money Maxwell had given her: to help her brother. That was one less secret to keep hidden.

Jago leaned closer to plant a soft kiss on her lips. 'Now, where was I?'

'You were about to make love to me, but I think I killed the mood,' Mollie said with a rueful grimace.

Jago took one of her hands and placed it on his swollen length. 'I'm always in the mood when it comes to you.' And he brought his mouth back down to hers to prove it.

After they both showered and changed, Jago took Mollie's hand in his to go to join his grandmother for afternoon tea. His body was still tingling from making love to Mollie both on the bed and again in the shower. He had to forcibly remind himself they were only pretending to be engaged. None of this was real, and yet he couldn't get enough of her. But asking her to consider taking this beyond the weekend was tricky. For one thing, there was the press attention their reunion would attract. He had enough trouble as it was trying to escape the intrusion of the tabloids. Secondly, if his grandmother made a full recovery, she would find out he had lied to her. Gran had spent years putting up with her husband's lies, and Jago hated to resemble his grandfather in any way, but what else could he do? He wanted what might well be his grandmother's last birthday to be happy, surrounded by her family. He wanted her to believe he was settling down at last. It would comfort her to know at least one of her three playboy grandsons was getting married. It was a pity Jonas couldn't be here to join the celebrations, but that was his brother's choice, and he had to accept it, even if it stirred a niggling worry that Jonas was not usually this long away on a mission.

Jago opened the door to the Green Room to find his grandmother sitting on a recliner near the window overlooking the garden. The tea tray hadn't yet been brought in, but he wanted his grandmother to see Mollie before the staff came in with the afternoon tea.

'Hey, Gran,' he said, leading Mollie into the room. 'Mollie is here to celebrate your birthday with you.'

Gran looked up and smiled, her eyes lighting up when her gaze rested on Mollie's beautiful face. She clasped her hands together like a young girl and exclaimed, 'Mollie, darling. How wonderful to see you. Come closer so I can kiss you. I'm afraid I'm not very mobile at present.'

Mollie came over and bent down to give his gran a gentle hug and a sweet kiss on both of her wrinkled cheeks. It made Jago's heart swell to see the enthusiasm and joy in his gran's face. And to witness what looked like the genuine affection Mollie exhibited for his grandmother.

'It's so lovely to see you too,' Mollie said, still holding on to one of the old lady's hands. 'How is your arm?'

Gran gave her arm in a cast a rolled-eye glance. 'It doesn't hurt now, but it's inconvenient, even though

I'm out of the sling. I can't do the things I want to do. I feel like a doddering old fool for tripping over in the garden. Or at least that's what I've been told I did. I don't remember a thing about it. All I remember is going out to get some daffodils for the breakfast room. I love this time of year, don't you?'

'I certainly do, and daffodils are one of my favourite flowers,' Mollie said and sat on the window seat close to Elsie's chair. The filtered sunlight coming in made Mollie's hair look like spun silk, and a frisson passed over Jago's flesh as he thought of how her hair had felt as he ran his fingers through it only half an hour before.

'I love them too,' Elsie said. 'Yellow is such a bright and positive colour.'

'I'm so sorry you hurt yourself, especially so close to your birthday,' Mollie said.

The woman smiled, her eyes sparkling. 'To tell you the truth, Mollie, I'm quite enjoying being waited on hand and foot. Now, tell me about you. How are the wedding plans going?'

A panicked look crossed Mollie's face for a nanosecond, and then she glanced at Jago. *Help me*, her eyes seemed to say.

Jago came and sat beside her on the window seat, taking her hand in both of his. 'They're going well, Gran. We're just waiting for Jonas to get back from the States. Do you remember he's over there working on a big top-secret naval project?'

Gran screwed up her face as if trying to put pieces

of a complicated puzzle together in her mind. She put a hand to her right temple and then shook her head in a self-disparaging way. 'I have such gaps in my memory these days…' She lowered her hand to her lap and smiled indulgently again at them both. 'You two look very much in love. I'm so looking forward to seeing you married.' She aimed her gaze at Mollie and added, 'I always knew Jago would only ever settle for someone who loved him as he deserves to be loved.' Her expression became wistful, and she continued. 'His father was madly in love with his mother, some would say too much so, but I don't agree. How can you love someone too much?'

'I guess it's better than not loving at all,' Mollie said without glancing Jago's way, but he suspected her comment was a dig at him for not being in love with her when he had proposed to her. But marriage had seemed the right way to go. He'd wanted her, he'd enjoyed her company, and he had pictured a mostly satisfying life together. Unromantic of him, sure, but he didn't have it in him to say those three little words out loud. Maybe he was incapable of romantic love. He had avoided it for his entire adult life, settling for casual flings rather than anything permanent. Until Mollie. But his feelings about her were difficult to define. He put his attraction to her down to lust, and while that still pulsed and throbbed between them, there was a new quality to it now. An intense quality that made him feel a deeper connection to her as if their lovemaking had shifted to another level of intimacy.

'So true...' Elsie looked into the distance as if recalling her early years with Jago's grandfather. His grandparents had been married a long time, but he wasn't sure his grandfather was even capable of the love Elsie had shown him. Her loyalty and faithfulness, for one thing, had not been returned in equal measure, and Maxwell had controlled every aspect of her life to the point where she hadn't even been allowed to properly grieve her son and daughter-in-law. There were no photos of Jago's father around the manor; they had been locked away soon after the accident.

Harriet brought in the tea tray at that point, and Jago rose from the window seat to help his grandmother by placing her cup of tea and a piece of her favourite cake close to where she was sitting.

'Thank you, dear,' Elsie said, smiling up at him.

Jago handed Mollie a cup of tea, and she took it from him with a smile that faltered around the edges. 'Piece of cake? Scone?' he asked, indicating the luscious spread Harriet had prepared.

'Just the tea, thank you.' The cup rattled against the saucer in Mollie's hand, and he laid a gentle hand on her shoulder to reassure her. It was a big ask to pretend to be madly in love with him when there was so much murky water under the bridge between them, but this weekend was important, and Jago was determined to see it through. It wasn't hard to pretend to be in love with her, especially after their lovemaking earlier.

Are you pretending?

His conscience gave him a mocking nudge, but he wasn't prepared to examine his feelings too closely. He had planned this weekend on the pretext of making his grandmother happy, but he knew deep down it hadn't been his sole motivation. He had wanted to see Mollie again. That was what he had wanted for the last two painful years—to see her, to ask her what had motivated her to jilt him. To prove to himself he could move on without her in his life. But the thought of not seeing her again after this weekend was beginning to torture him. He shied away from it, tried not to imagine how lonely he would be without her in his life.

'Is my grandfather joining us?' Jago asked Harriet as she prepared to leave the room.

'No, he will see you at dinner,' Harriet said. 'He had his physical therapist here this morning so he's feeling tired.'

'Your grandfather isn't one for socialising these days,' Elsie said to Jago with a rueful grimace.

'How has he been?' Jago asked, absently stirring his sugarless cup of tea for something to do with his hands. Sitting so close to Mollie was making him distracted like a horny teenager. All he wanted to do was touch her. His blood was still thrumming with the excitement of possessing her earlier. He had to drag his eyes away from her every time she took a sip of her tea, those luscious lips around the rim of her china cup sending his pulse sky-high.

'Oh, you know your grandfather, dear,' Gran said with a sad shake of her head. 'He's finding his limitations so terribly frustrating.'

'You have limitations too, but you don't grumble about them,' Jago pointed out.

Elsie put her cup and saucer down with a sigh. 'I guess I'm used to being limited.' She turned her gaze to Mollie's and added, 'Now, let's talk about the wedding. I've forgotten all the details since my fall, but Harriet assured me that I was helping you plan it. Is the cake sorted?'

'Yep, all sorted,' Jago said, wryly thinking of the wedding cake and Mollie's dress at his London apartment.

'I can't wait to see your dress,' Gran said. 'But we mustn't talk about it in front of the groom. It's bad luck.' She leaned forward to pat Jago's hand. 'Would you mind if Mollie and I had a bit of time together catching up? You could go and check on your grandfather, take him a slice of this delicious lemon drizzle cake. But no cream. It's not good for him.'

Mollie's eyes widened a fraction at his gran's suggestion of a private tete-a-tete with her, but Jago gave her a reassuring wink and took a slice of the cake from the tea tray. He bent down and planted a kiss on Mollie's soft lips, breathing in the sweet scent of her, before lifting his mouth away. 'I'll see you at dinner, if not before.'

'You're making the poor girl blush,' Gran said with mock reproval, but there was a sparkle in her eyes all the same.

Once Jago had left the room, Mollie put her teacup and saucer on the table in front of the window seat. 'Can I pour you another cup of tea?' she asked Elsie, to fill the sudden silence.

'No, thank you, dear,' Elsie said with a gentle smile. 'Now, how are you?' There was suddenly a piercing set to the old lady's gaze that was a little unnerving.

'I—I'm fine, thank you,' Mollie said, trying not to sound as flustered as she felt.

'Not getting wedding jitters, are we?'

Mollie swallowed tightly. 'Erm...should I be?'

Elsie gave a wistful smile. 'I was frightfully nervous before my wedding. Back in those days, of course, Maxwell and I didn't spend much time together alone, if you know what I mean.' She looked down at the rings on her left hand—a wedding, engagement and eternity ring that were probably worth more than most people earned in a lifetime. Elsie's gaze came back up to meet Mollie's once more. 'Jago is nothing like his grandfather. He might be ruthless in business, as are all three of my grandsons, but he's a good man. He'll make an excellent father. Do you want children?'

Mollie was a little blindsided by the question.

'Erm...yes, maybe one day, I guess. I wouldn't want to rush into it, though.'

Elsie put a hand on Mollie's knee and gave it a gentle pat. 'You'll be a wonderful mother, I'm sure.'

'I don't know about that,' Mollie suddenly found herself confessing. 'I didn't have the best role model in my own mother.'

Elsie looked at her with kind eyes full of compassion. 'Do you still have her?'

'No, she died when I was six.'

'And your father?'

'I've never met him. He abandoned my mother before I was born.'

Elsie sighed and placed her hand back in her lap. 'No wonder you and Jago fell in love. You have a lot in common, both losing parents so young.' She blinked a couple of times as if trying to hold back tears. Tears that were not allowed to be shed all those years ago.

'It must have been a terrible time for you when you lost your son and daughter-in-law,' Mollie said softly.

'Oh, it was,' Elsie said looking down at her hands. 'But I had three grieving little boys to take care of, so there was no time for me to dwell on things.' She looked up at Mollie again with a smile that was a little forced. 'Of course, Maxwell thinks I'm a sentimental old fool for still getting teary on James's birthday every year, but I miss him to this day. He and Alice would be so proud of their boys. They've done well for themselves in spite of...everything.'

Mollie had a feeling *everything* included how their

grandfather had raised them with an iron fist and a heart of steel. 'I think you've been a wonderful grandmother to them, and they're so fortunate to have you.' Her voice came out raspy, and there was a lump in her throat.

Elsie reached for Mollie's left hand and looked down at the engagement ring glinting on her ring finger. 'Such a beautiful ring and a beautiful choice of bride. Jago has excellent taste.'

But I'm a fake, and so is the ring.

'I'm terrified I'm going to lose it,' Mollie said.

Elsie met her gaze with unwavering focus. 'Rings can be replaced, people cannot.' Then she gave Mollie's hand a gentle squeeze, and her tone lightened. 'I'm looking forward to the wedding. Ever since I woke up after my silly fall, it's all I can think about. For a horrible moment there when I woke up in the emergency room, I thought I'd missed it.' She gave a tinkling laugh and shook her head in a self-effacing manner. 'But Jago assured me I hadn't.'

Mollie disguised another tight swallow. 'No. You haven't missed it.'

Because it never happened, and now it never will.

CHAPTER NINE

MOLLIE WAS ON her way back to the room she was sharing with Jago when she came to the library. As stately home libraries went, Wildewood Manor's was one of the best, but it was spoiled for her now as it was the place where Maxwell Wilde had presented her with his ultimatum two years ago. The library door was ajar, and she found herself moving towards it like an automaton, drawn to the space in spite of the memories it would evoke. She listened for any sound, but it was so quiet she could hear the soft ticking of a carriage clock in the sitting room opposite. Mollie gingerly opened the door a little farther and checked no one was in there. Finding it empty, she let out a sigh of relief and stepped over the threshold, pulling the door to behind her. The click of the lock was still faintly audible, and she stood stock-still, breathing in the scent of the ancient books that lined three walls of the cavernous room.

It was like stepping through a portal into another world, a world before phones and computers and emails. It was a dark room due to the wood panelling and floor-to-ceiling shelves and heavy brocade curtains hanging from the windows, but on this occasion, the curtains were only half-drawn to keep the afternoon light off the priceless tomes.

There was an extendable ladder set against one section of the bookshelves for gaining access to the books on the top shelves. There was a large leather-topped walnut desk to one side of the room with a leather chair set behind it. On the desk was a brass gooseneck reading lamp, a leather-bound journal of some sort, a gold fountain pen and even an old-fashioned quill, adding to the old-world atmosphere.

Mollie moved towards the desk and absently turned the swivel chair, watching as it went full circle...not unlike her, back at Wildewood Manor as Jago's fiancée. Pretending but feeling real emotions that—just like two years ago—were not returned by Jago. How could they be? Even if he had fallen in love with her, it was the other version of herself she had presented, not who she was now. But she sensed Jago was closer to her now than before, and she certainly felt closer to him, even though he had given her no guarantee of a future with him. Why would he? She had jilted him once. Would he risk it again? Unlikely.

There was a whirring sound from the shadows of the great room, and Mollie's heart leapt to her throat as Maxwell Wilde glided out into the light in his electric wheelchair.

'So you're back.' His faded blue eyes scanned her critically, his voice hard, his mouth tight, his bushy salt-and-pepper eyebrows fused in a frown of disapproval.

Mollie schooled her features into a calm facade, but inside she was quaking like a child in front of a stern schoolmaster. Her heart swung in her chest like an out-of-control pendulum, and she grasped the back of the leather chair to keep herself steady as her legs were like half-set jelly. Maxwell Wilde might be somewhat diminished since his stroke a year ago, but he still had a lot of power at his fingertips, power that could destroy her and those she loved.

'Jago insisted I came for his grandmother's birthday. I'm assuming he didn't check that was okay with you first?' She kept her voice as cool as her expression, so cool it could have frosted the windows.

Maxwell activated his chair to cross the acre of carpet, coming farther out of the shadows to glare at her. 'Since her fall, my wife has forgotten what you did to our grandson.'

Mollie ground her back teeth, fighting with every cell of her being not to be intimidated by him. 'I would never have jilted him if it hadn't been for—'

'I forbid you to speak of it.' He held up his hand like a stop sign. 'That was our agreement, was it not? It must not be mentioned again.'

Mollie flattened her lips into a tight line, staring down at him with anger pounding in her blood with hammers of hatred. 'Jago knows about the money you gave me to go away. He didn't hear it from me. He found out by himself.'

Maxwell's jaw tightened like a vice, and his eyes hardened to steel. 'You're fortunate he doesn't know why I paid you to go.' He rested his elbows on the armrests of his chair and steepled his fingers, watching her like a bird of prey.

Mollie held his gaze with gritty determination. 'Will you tell him?'

A devilish glint appeared in his eyes. 'Not unless you get any fancy ideas of becoming part of this family.'

'I can't see that happening,' Mollie said, her heart contracting. 'Jago will never forgive me for jilting him.'

'Nor should he,' Maxwell said, unlocking his fingers to grasp the armrests of his chair. 'You lied to him from the start, pretending to be someone you're not. I will not have the Wilde name polluted by the likes of you.'

Mollie stiffened her spine in pride. She had suffered from bullies since childhood and refused to be a soft target any more. She was not to blame for her circumstances of birth. It wasn't her fault her mother had not been up to the task of parenting her and her half-brother. 'I might not have the pedigree you would desire your grandson to join with in marriage, but I loved Jago will all my heart.'

Maxwell made a scoffing sound. 'If you loved him, you would have been honest with him instead of whitewashing your less than desirable background.'

Mollie gave him a challenging stare. 'You are not someone I will tolerate a lecture on honesty from.'

Maxwell's bushy brows rose in an imperious arc, but she read a mark of respect in his gaze she had never seen before. 'Ah, so you do have some spirit. Tell me, what did you do with the money I gave you?'

'I spent it on getting my half-brother into long-term rehab.'

'Did it work?'

Mollie let out a long breath, her shoulders slumping in spite of her efforts to maintain a rigid and defensive posture. 'Not yet.'

'But you refuse to give up hope?' He delivered it as a statement, not a question, his expression inscrutable.

'I figure while he is alive, there is hope. It's what keeps me going.'

'Optimistic of you.'

'Perhaps, but I can't live my life any other way.'

There was a silence measured only by the sound of a breeze that had whipped up outside, making a scratching sound from the leaves on the trees against the windows.

'Let's hope that optimism doesn't include any plans to reunite with my grandson,' Maxwell said. 'I will allow this little game of charades for Elsie's sake, but that's as far as it must go.'

'How magnanimous of you,' Mollie said with a touch of asperity. 'I'll enjoy making the most of it.'

Maxwell's eyes went to the ring on her left hand before he met her gaze once more with a cynical smile. 'Don't get too attached to that ring, will you.'

Mollie glanced down at the ring and then curled

her fingers into her palm and met his gaze with a defiant glare. 'Contrary to what you believe about me, I value people, not worldly goods. Anyway, this ring is a fake, like my current relationship with Jago.'

Maxwell gave her a penetrating look as if he was reassessing her. Hardly a muscle moved on his face, and yet she got the impression he had come to a new opinion about her. One that challenged his view of her as a social-climbing gold-digger.

Mollie held his look, coming to a decision that gave her a way out of Maxwell's hold over her. She had not broken the NDA, and she now, thanks to Jago, had the money to pay Maxwell back. He could no longer control her as long as the images had been destroyed. That was a risk she would have to take, because otherwise she would never escape this nightmare. People had controlled her all her life, and she was not allowing it any more. 'I now have enough money to pay you back. You might control Elsie and your grandsons, but you are not going to control me.'

'Aren't you forgetting something?' Maxwell said with a vulpine look that chilled her to the marrow.

There was a creak as the library door opened and Jago appeared. He took in the tense tableau with an assessing glance then stepped farther into the room, coming over to Mollie and addressing his grandfather. 'What are you talking about?'

Maxwell's jaw was so tight it looked like it might crack like concrete under the pressure of old tree roots. 'Why have you brought her back here? She jilted you, for God's sake. And she's violating our agreement on the payout which, I might remind you, she grabbed with greedy gold-digging hands.'

Jago stood close to Mollie without touching her, but she drew strength from the solid warmth of his body. 'I don't believe Mollie is a gold-digger. I don't think I ever totally believed it. She put that money to good use to help her brother.'

Maxwell curled his top lip. 'A brother who is a drug addict and a drunk. I don't want our name dragged into the gutter by people who can't control their urges and obsessions.'

'I think you're the one who is obsessed,' Mollie said. 'You're obsessed with controlling everyone in your life. But there will come a day when you won't be able to do it any more.'

Maxwell glared at her like he wanted to vaporise on her the spot. 'I can still control you, and you damn well know it.'

Mollie stared him down with a source of courage she hadn't known she possessed. 'There's nothing else you can take from me. I'm not going to be manipulated again.' Then with a brief glance at Jago, she swept out of the room with stately self-possession, closing the door with a hard snick as she left.

Jago was torn between wanting to follow Mollie and wanting to find out what his grandfather had alluded to during the conversation he had overheard as he entered the library. 'Was that necessary?' he asked with a frown. 'I brought Mollie here for Gran's sake.'

'Did she ask for money to come?'

'I made her an offer, otherwise I'm sure she would never have come here.'

'She's not good for you, Jago. You were lucky to escape her, believe me. You were becoming obsessed with her. That's not something I want for you.'

Jago stared down at his grandfather. 'Isn't what I want for me more important than what you want for me? I'm no longer a child under your care—if you could call how you raised us as *care*, that is.'

'What's that supposed to mean?' Maxwell sniped with a brooding scowl. 'I provided for you. I took you boys under my own roof. I paid for your education, and you wanted for nothing.'

Except my parents...and unconditional love and acceptance.

The realisation had always been in his mind, but Jago had stored it at the back where he couldn't think about it too much. But he hadn't been allowed to think about, much less vocalise, the trauma of losing his parents. He and his brothers had been provided for generously in a financial sense but not in terms of love, especially not from their grandfather. Their grandmother did her best while swamped in her own grief for her adored son and daughter-in-law. Jago wondered if her memory loss now was somehow related to that unresolved grief. Her mind was stuck on what was for her a rare happy time in her life: the impending marriage of her middle grandson to Mollie Cassidy.

Jago was starting to put the pieces of a complicated puzzle together, and he wasn't sure he liked what he saw. His grandfather's set against Mollie was out of all proportion. It didn't make any sense. Yes, his grandfather was an appalling snob and looked down on those less fortunate than himself, but Maxwell's treatment of Mollie begged further examination. Jago had the power now to look deeper into his grandfather's affairs to see if there was something Maxwell had over Mollie that she hadn't revealed to him. Was her continued silence because of that wretched NDA? How could he get her to open up to him? To trust him? She hadn't trusted him two years ago; instead, she had bolted after being paid to leave by his grandfather. Jago understood her commitment to her half-brother, although he wasn't particularly close to his own brothers. Their grandfather had made sure of that.

Jago looked down at his grandfather again, fighting the urge to tell him what he really thought of him. But Maxwell was old and frail and didn't have half the power he thought he had over him now. 'I'm going to Mollie. We will discuss this further at some other point.'

Maxwell gripped the arms of his chair, his bony knuckles showing white as the pebbles on the driveway outside the manor. 'Don't make a fool of yourself over that girl all over again,' he barked, his rheumy eyes flashing with barely contained rage. 'Your father was obsessed with your mother, and look how that played out.'

An echoing silence bounced off the walls of the library.

'I'm not obsessed with Mollie, nor am I in love with her,' Jago said, but something inside his chest prodded his heart like a long thin needle sending radiating pain throughout his body.

But out of habit, he ignored it.

Mollie was pacing the floor of their room upstairs, unable to settle to anything. Her emotions were in turmoil, and yet she was proud of how she had stood up to Maxwell Wilde. It would remain to be seen what he did next, but she reassured herself her brother was safe for now. She had used her phone app to repay Maxwell every penny of his disgusting payout, and in doing so a load had come off her shoulders.

Jago entered the room just as she was doing another circuit, and she swung around to face him. His expression was apologetic, and it gave her hope that some of his walls were coming down.

'I'm sorry about the way my grandfather spoke to you,' he said, raking a hand through his hair in a manner she had come to recognise as a signal of distress. 'It was unforgivable.'

'You've called me the same,' Mollie pointed out, not quite ready to let him off the hook.

'I know, and I don't expect you to forgive me, but I don't think any such thing now.' He moved across to where she was standing, not reaching for her but close enough for her to be drawn into his magnetic field. Her body craved his touch, longed for him to take her in his arms and provide the comfort and shelter she had been praying for her entire life.

Mollie couldn't take her eyes off his bottomless blue ones. They were so deep and dark like the sky on a moonless night. She ran the tip of her tongue over her lips and watched as his gaze followed its movement. The air tightened. Electric energy crackled in the atmosphere. Her body tingled from head to foot, and she stepped closer at the same time he did. Their bodies collided, his arms came around her, tightly, possessively, greedily, and his mouth came down on hers in a kiss that sent a rocket blast of lust through her flesh. He groaned something unintelligible against her lips then deepened the kiss with a commanding thrust of his tongue that mimicked the primal act she knew was coming next. She wanted him with a feverish hunger that pounded in her blood, and she could feel the same need in him as he crushed her against his thickened length.

'I want you. Now.' He said the words in an agonised way, his hands cupping her bottom to hold her even closer to his pulsing need, the same need she could feel thundering in her own body.

'I want you too,' Mollie said, tearing at his shirt like it was crepe paper. A button popped, and she heard it ping to the floor. 'Sorry, I'm ruining your expensive shirt.'

'I couldn't care less about my freaking shirt,' he growled and set to work on her clothes as she continued with his.

In a matter of seconds, they were both naked on the bed in a tangle of limbs. Jago pushed back her hair from her forehead, looking deeply into her eyes. 'When I decided to bring you here for Gran's birthday, I didn't expect this to happen between us.' He frowned and added, 'I didn't want you to feel any obligation to sleep with me.'

Mollie lifted one of her hands to his face, stroking his lean jaw, delighting in the rasp of his stubble against her softer skin. 'I told myself I wouldn't allow you to lay a finger on me, but somehow I underestimated the way your touch would make me feel.'

He gave a crooked smile and leaned closer to press a light-as-air kiss to her lips. He lifted his mouth off hers and cupped one side of her face in his broad hand, his thumb stroking back and forth in a tender caress. 'Same goes. Which brings me to the question of what we're going to do about it.'

Mollie wasn't confident enough to ask what he meant so stayed silent, watching him as he surveyed her face as if memorising every one of her features.

Jago took her chin between his thumb and index finger, holding her gaze intently. 'Do you have any suggestions?'

Mollie disguised a swallow, not sure where he was going with their relationship but aching to know. 'I'm not sure your grandfather would be happy to know we're sleeping together.'

His brows came together in a savage frown. 'Can we for once leave my grandfather out of it? He's done enough damage as it is.'

And he can do so much more.

Mollie lifted her finger to his frown and tried to smooth it away. 'Make love to me, Jago. Please?'

Jago let out a rough-edged sigh and gathered her close once more. 'With the greatest of pleasure.' And his mouth came back to hers in a kiss that sent hot shivers down her spine.

His lovemaking was fast, urgent, desperate as if he knew the clock was ticking on their relationship. Mollie responded to him with the same urgency and desperation, not wanting to think too far ahead for there, surely, lay heartbreak. Jago might say he wanted her, and he demonstrated it convincingly, but he had never told her his feelings about her. He had never mentioned the word *love*, only *lust*. Would it be enough for her to accept him on those terms, even if he only offered a temporary fling? She couldn't think about it now, not while his mouth was working its mind-blowing magic on hers. Not while his hands were touching her, shaping her, caressing her until she was panting with need.

This was always what worked between them—the sexual energy that fired between them. The intensity of it had grown, not lessened, which gave breath to her hopes, making her fall under the sensual spell of his lovemaking all over again.

CHAPTER TEN

THE BIRTHDAY PARTY for Elsie, while small by Wilde standards, was no less glamorous. Instead of using the ballroom, the garden room was set up with beautiful flower arrangements and balloons and streamers and a banner with *Happy Birthday* on the wall above the spectacular birthday cake. While the last touches were being made by the staff, Mollie went upstairs to get ready. She dressed with care, pleased with the way her blue dress hadn't dated and showcased her slim build and the grey-blue of her eyes. She put her hair up in a stylish bun, leaving a couple of tendrils to dance around her face. She was putting the finishing touches to her make-up when Jago came in.

'You look stunning,' he said coming over to drop a kiss to her bare shoulder, his eyes meeting hers in the mirror.

'So do you.' Mollie drank in his handsome features, his dress suit highlighting his tall, broad-shouldered frame and athletic build to perfection.

'I have something for you.' He opened his jacket

to take out a slim rectangular jewellery box the same colour as his eyes.

Mollie took it from him, her heart skipping in her chest. She prised open the lid to find a gorgeous sapphire pendant, surrounded by sparkling diamonds and a pair of dangling earrings to match. 'Oh…they're beautiful…' She met his gaze in the mirror once more. 'Are they…real?'

He gave a short laugh. 'Of course they're real. Here, I'll help you with the pendant.' He took the box from her and took out the necklace, placing it around her neck and fastening it. 'You'd better do the earrings yourself.' He handed her each one in turn as she put them on.

Mollie stared at herself in the mirror, feeling like Cinderella dressed for the ball. The earrings sparkled as they moved, the pendant's sapphire as dark as the ring on her left hand. 'I'll give them back once the party is over.'

'No need to,' Jago said. 'Consider it a gift.'

'But, Jago, these are so expensive. I can't possibly accept such a—'

His hands came down on her shoulders, sending shivers of reaction through her body. 'I want you to have them.' There was an implacable quality to his voice and a determined look in his eyes.

She rose from the chair she was sitting on and turned to face him. Her thoughts were tumbling like leaves in a whirlwind. 'When did you buy these?'

Something moved at the backs of his eyes. 'Why do you want to know?'

'Because it's important.'

'It's just a bit of jewellery.'

'When?' Mollie persisted.

Jago let out a rough sigh. 'I bought them two years ago while I was in New York. They were going to be a gift for our wedding day.'

Mollie bit down on her lower lip, her heart contracting at the thought of how much she had hurt him back then. 'You kept them all this time?' Her voice came out as a scratchy whisper.

He gave a dismissive shrug. 'Who else was I going to give them to?'

'You've had those five lovers since...haven't you?'

He stepped away as if he needed some space, one of his hands raking through his hair, leaving it tousled. 'I didn't date anyone for the first year.'

Shock, surprise and relief washed over her. 'No one?'

His expression became wry. 'I shelved my playboy lifestyle for twelve months, then I began a few flings but...' He gave another shrug and went on. 'It wasn't the same. I wasn't the same.'

Mollie blinked back the moisture in her eyes. 'I don't know if this is any comfort to you, but I haven't slept with anyone since we broke up.'

Jago's eyes widened a fraction. 'No one?'

'No one.'

He came over to her and took her hands in his,

drawing her closer to his body. 'Why?' His gaze was searching, a deep frown pulling at his brow.

Mollie let out a soft sigh. 'Lots of reasons. I had my brother to look after. I had to find a new job, a place to live. There's not been time for anything else.'

And I didn't want anyone but you.

She wanted to say it, but what good would it do now?

Jago lifted her chin with the tip of his finger, his gaze still locked on hers. 'We'd better not be late for Gran's party, but this conversation isn't over. My grandfather was behind you leaving me, and if you won't tell me what led you to do it, I'll have to find out some other way. It can't have just been your brother's issues.'

Mollie pressed her lips together to stop herself blurting out the truth. If she told him, she would be breaking the terms of the non-disclosure agreement and risking Maxwell retaliating by releasing the images.

The guests were still arriving as Mollie and Jago entered the party room hand in hand. Mollie could see Jack, Jago's older brother, leaning down to kiss Elsie. He straightened to his full height and glanced Mollie's way. His dark eyebrows rose a fraction, and he sauntered over with his mouth smiling with welcome, but his ice-blue eyes had a cynical glint.

'Welcome back into the Wilde fold, Mollie,' he said with a mock bow. He turned to Jago and added,

'What did the old man think of you two getting back together?'

Jago's mouth flattened into a thin line of tension. 'He's not happy, but I'm only concerned with Gran at the moment. She's thrilled to see Mollie.'

'Yeah, so I just heard.' Jack rubbed at his jaw in a thoughtful manner. 'I don't buy it, you know.'

Jago frowned. 'What do you mean?'

'I think Gran remembers more than she's letting on,' Jack said.

'You've been a lawyer way too long,' Jago said, but he was still frowning. 'Her memory is patchy, sure, but she thinks we're still planning the wedding.'

Jack's smile was as cynical as his eyes. 'And are you?'

Jago's hand tightened as it held Mollie's. 'No,' Jago said. 'This is just for the weekend.'

Jack's gaze went to the jewellery around Mollie's neck and the earrings dangling from her ears before glancing at the ring on her left hand. 'Given the amount of money you've spent, I'd be stringing it out a bit longer to get value for money.'

Jago muttered a thick curse word. 'Keep your opinions to yourself, Jack. I know what I'm doing.'

Jack gave a careless shrug, and with another mercurial smile directed at Mollie, he strolled away to speak to some of the other guests.

Jago turned to Mollie. 'I'm sorry about Jack. He's always been a bit of a pot-stirrer.'

'It's okay. I know the terms of our deal.' Mollie

glanced in Elsie's direction to see her chatting with some old friends. She turned back to Jago. 'But what if your gran does remember?'

'I'll cross that bridge if and when I need to. But for now, why don't we go and get some fresh air?' He led her out through the French door that opened to the garden, taking her past a maze to a summer house enveloped in white clematis. Bees were busily buzzing, and birds were twittering, and the afternoon sunlight cast everything in a golden glow.

Jago looked back at the manor where the party was continuing without them. He was frowning when he turned to look at Mollie. 'This weekend might not be enough.'

Mollie licked her suddenly dry lips. 'What do you mean?'

'We might need to continue our relationship for a little longer than I anticipated.'

'How much longer?'

'Jack could be right about Gran. She may well remember more than we thought, but I don't want to upset her by suddenly ending our relationship when she's clearly thrilled we're back together.'

'I'm not sure your grandfather is going to be happy about that,' Mollie said, biting down on her lip.

Jago's frown carved deep into his forehead. 'Why is he anything to do with us?'

'He's everything to do with us,' she said before she could put the brakes on her tongue.

He squeezed her hands. 'Tell me everything, Mollie, please. I'm determined to find out either way, but it would be better if I heard it from you.'

'You know I can't say anything. I signed a—'

'Screw the NDA. This is about us. It's about you learning to trust me, damn it.'

Mollie pulled out of his hold as the music coming from the house signalled it was cake-cutting time. 'We'd better go back. It will look strange if we're not there to sing "Happy Birthday" to your gran.'

Jago let out a savage sigh and walked with her back to the manor in silence. The party had livened up, and people were gathering for the blowing out of the candles. Mollie put her on best party smile, but it took an effort to keep it in place. What did Jago want from her? A fling? A proper relationship? To try again? He hadn't said anything about his feelings. Their relationship was based on lust just as it had been two years ago. Wouldn't she be making the same mistake to settle for anything less than love?

After his grandmother blew out her candles, with some help from Jack, Maxwell rolled up to make a speech on his wife's behalf. While he was thanking all the guests for coming and being as charming as a wily fox, Jago took the opportunity to slip away to look for the answer to the question that was playing on his mind. Why did Mollie accept the payout from his grandfather to jilt him? It surely couldn't have been solely about getting help for her brother, although he knew long-term rehab was expensive and repeated sessions were not unusual. He went to his grandfather's private study which, unsurprisingly, was locked, but fortunately he knew where a spare key was planted. His grandfather resented Jago having access to his business records, but since Maxwell's stroke, Jago had made it his mission to check every detail in case of discrepancies. His grandfather wasn't as sharp as he used to be, and Jago had already found a couple of accounting mistakes that would have created a tax nightmare if not corrected in time. He logged into his grandfather's computer to access his financial transactions, searching for the payment Maxwell had made to Mollie two years ago. It wasn't the first time Jago had seen it, but this time he stared at it, his mind ticking through the possibilities. There were no records of any emails from Maxwell to Mollie, and yet he felt sure there must have been some communication other than in person. He couldn't search his grandfather's phone because he had seen Maxwell use it to read the speech he had composed for his wife. Jago rifled through the drawers of the desk, trying to be fast yet tidy in his approach. His search proved fruitless, and he leaned back in the leather chair and let out a sigh of frustration.

Then he remembered the safe hidden behind the bookshelves. It was where his grandfather kept large sums of cash and some of Gran's most valuable jewellery. Jago didn't know the combination, but on a whim, he tried his father's birthday and year of birth, and the safe opened. Inside was an astonishing amount of cash and some jewellery, and right at the back was a phone. He took it out and saw that that the battery was dead, so he hunted around for a charger. He found one in a drawer of a filing cabinet and quickly plugged it in, waiting impatiently for it to charge enough for him to access it. The minutes dragged by, and he could hear the party in the background and hoped no one would come looking for him. Finally, the phone had enough charge for Jago to turn it on. Of course, it had another code but after three tries he cracked it with Jack's birthday and year of birth.

Jago scrolled through the messages, and his eyes rounded when he saw one from his grandfather to Mollie. There were pictures attached and he clicked on them, his stomach churning when he saw the explicit images of Mollie. He had seen her naked, had made intimate love with her many times, but he had never seen her in such provocative poses. It was so out of character. The images were nothing short of pornographic. Was this part of her past she was keen to keep hidden? How had his grandfather come across them? Had he used them to get her to jilt him? Nothing made any sense…other than Mollie hadn't come to him and explained her dilemma but instead had chosen to bolt, leaving him virtually standing at the altar. That stung more than anything. She hadn't turned to him but had accepted money from his meddling grandfather to go away.

Mollie was finding it hard to make small talk with some of the guests. She felt like a fraud, pretending to be reunited with Jago when the truth was she was on borrowed time. She looked around for him, but he had disappeared during his grandfather's speech. Not that he had missed much. The words Maxwell spoke were hardly what anyone in the know would call *sincere*. But Maxwell Wilde was a showman, and he worked the room, making the small gathering of friends believe he was a devoted husband. She wanted to vomit.

Mollie made good her escape when the dancing began. She had never felt less like partying. She was on her way back to her and Jago's room when she saw him come out of his grandfather's office. There was a thunderous scowl on his face, and his eyes were dark blue flint.

'I want to talk to you. In private.' His words were clipped, his mouth set in a tense line.

'So talk.'

'Not here. Come into the library.'

Mollie followed him into the library a few doors down from the study. Once they were both inside, Jago closed the door with a resounding click then walked over to stand in front of her. 'Why didn't you tell me about the images?'

Mollie stared at him in shock, her heart beating so

heavily she could feel her hammering blood in her fingertips. 'You've seen them?' she asked without a thought for the NDA. Shame coursed through her that Jago, the man she loved, had seen her in such degrading poses. And even though strictly speaking it wasn't actually her in those pictures, it still felt like she could never escape their black mark against her.

'I found a burner phone of my grandfather's just now.'

'They're not me,' Mollie said. 'They're deepfakes. I don't know where your grandfather found them—he didn't tell me. He just told me that someone was going to release them if he didn't pay the ransom to keep them out of the press. But the deal was I had to leave and never contact you.'

Jago's frown was so deep it dug a trench between his eyes. 'But why didn't you come to me? I was about to become your husband. Why would you allow my grandfather to convince you to—'

Tears welled in Mollie's eyes, her heart aching like it was being compressed in a vice. 'I had to protect my brother, but also I was thinking of you.'

'Thinking of me?' Jago snapped back. 'By jilting me the day before the wedding? How was that in my best interests?' Bitterness laced his tone, and his gaze was as searing as a laser beam.

Mollie hugged her arms around her trembling body. 'You were negotiating that big deal in New York. I was worried if those images were released to the press, you would lose the deal and your reputation would be tarnished by me. And I was worried about Eliot. He was fragile. He still is fragile. If he saw me being humiliated in every newspaper and social media platform, it could have tipped him over the edge. I couldn't risk it. Surely you can understand that?'

Jago swung away from her and raked a hand through his hair. He dropped his hand back by his side, but she noticed both of his hands were clenched. Tension and anger rippled across his features, but behind the fury she could see a glimpse of profound hurt he was at great pains to conceal. 'You promised to marry me, Mollie. You agreed to spend your life with me, and yet you didn't come to me when you needed help. You didn't trust me. You let my grandfather rescue you, but at what price to us?'

'It wasn't about the money, although I needed it desperately for Eliot.'

'I'm not calling you a gold-digger because you're clearly not,' Jago said, some of his anger softening in his voice. 'Your love and concern for your brother are truly admirable. But I still can't see why you didn't wait for me. I was only hours away from getting back from New York.'

Mollie glared back at him out of frustration. 'Do you know how quickly those images could have been uploaded?' She snapped her fingers for emphasis. 'That's how quickly. I didn't have hours to waste, I didn't have minutes. Your grandfather promised me it would all go away, and it did. I abided by the terms of his deal, and he did too. I paid him back the money using some of the money you gave me. He has nothing over me now.'

'But he still has the images.'

Jago's statement hit her like a punch. Somehow, she hadn't taken in everything Jago had told her about finding the images.

They still existed.

Lumps of ice chugged through her veins, and her legs shook until she wasn't sure she could stay upright. She reached blindly for the desk chair and sat down with an ungainly thump, turning her anguished face towards Jago. 'They weren't destroyed?'

'No.'

'But your grandfather assured me they would be. He said the ransom would take care of everything, that as long as I disappeared, those images would be gone.'

'He lied.'

Mollie swallowed and knotted her hands together until her fingers ached. 'So they still could be leaked?'

'Not if I can help it.' Determination underlined his tone. 'But there's one thing I don't understand. Why did the alleged blackmailer approach my grandfather and not me? I have just as much wealth and reputation to protect, and you were my fiancée.'

Mollie pushed herself out of the chair, wrapping her arms around her body once more. 'I've never understood that either, but you weren't marrying me for the right reasons, and I wonder now if your grandfather realised that.'

'All that aside, your first instinct was to lock me out, but this was your present unfolding in real time. I should have been the one to help you. You were the woman I had chosen to be my wife, for God's sake. But you left me completely in the dark.'

'You didn't love me. You never told me you loved me.'

Jago clamped down on his jaw. 'Words are not as important as actions.'

'Actions are fine, but I've never been told I was loved by anyone in my entire life.'

He drew in a rough-sounding breath, his expression locking down as if her words had triggered something painful in him. 'I can't talk about this now. I think we need to confront my grandfather to see where these images originated.'

Mollie frowned. 'Is now the best time? It's your grandmother's birthday. I don't want it ruined by an argument with your grandfather.' It occurred to her then that she was still in protection mode just as she had been all her life. Protecting herself, protecting her brother, giving up Jago to protect him two years ago, protecting his grandmother from any fallout after a confrontation with Maxwell. Mollie was twenty-eight years old and still using the same old strategies she'd used from childhood, trying to fix things and taking responsibility for others.

Jago pocketed the burner phone. 'Gran will need

a rest soon anyway. I'll see if I can get my grandfather to meet us in his study in half an hour.' He held out a hand to her. 'Come here.'

Mollie stepped forward, and he captured her hand and brought it up to his lips, pressing a barely there kiss to her fingertips. 'I shouldn't have allowed my business deal to take priority so close to our wedding. It left you in the firing line, and I wasn't there to protect you.'

Plenty of people had offered to protect her and failed to do so. She herself had promised to protect her brother but had tragically failed. But it warmed her heart to think Jago would have done so two years ago if only she had asked him for help. Mollie gave him a twisted smile tinged with regret. 'I'm not used to relying on anyone for protection.'

He gathered her closer and bent his head till his mouth was close to hers. 'Maybe it's time to start.' And he kissed her tenderly, passionately, until she was incapable of thought, only feeling. Being in Jago's arms, sheltered by his embrace was like coming home after a lifetime of wandering anchorless, lost, alone. Dared she hope that he cared more for her than he was prepared to admit?

CHAPTER ELEVEN

Jago returned with Mollie to the party but as he had anticipated, his grandmother was tiring and ready for a rest. Jack was in the process of helping her out of her chair, tucking her arm in his and gently leading her out of the room. His brother might be a hard-nosed divorce lawyer, but there was a softer side to him not many people witnessed. There was no sign of his grandfather, but some of the guests insisted on saying goodbye to him and Mollie, which delayed his mission to confront the old man.

'Congratulations on getting back together,' one of his grandmother's friends said with a beaming smile. 'I hope you'll be very happy together. Can't wait until the wedding—that is, if I'm invited again?'

'Of course you will be,' Jago said almost mechanically. But the idea stuck in his head like a thorn on a fine fabric, leaving its mark even when he pulled away from its grip. There was nothing to stop him marrying Mollie, not now he knew what had caused their break-up. He could make up for the last two years: he had enough money to give her a comfortable life, a secure and happy future. They were a good match, not just physically. Mollie understood him in ways a lot of people didn't. She understood the loss he had experienced because she had faced her own tragic losses. He felt a connection with her he hadn't felt with anyone else. Surely that was a good basis for a long-term partnership?

Finally, the last guests left, and Jago asked Harriet where his grandfather was.

'He's out in the garden by the fountain. Jim took him out a while back for some fresh air,' she said. 'He goes out most afternoons at this time if the weather is fine.'

'Thanks,' Jago said, taking Mollie's hand in his. 'If you see Jim, ask him to wait until I've finished talking to my grandfather in private.'

'Will do, Mr Jago,' Harriet said and smiled at Mollie. 'I hope you enjoyed the party. Lady Wilde was so delighted to see you it was all she could talk about. It's given her such a boost.'

'It was a lovely party and the food was delicious,' Mollie said with a smile. 'Thank you for all your hard work.'

'It's my pleasure,' Harriet said with another smile then excusing herself went off to finish clearing the tables.

Jago led Mollie out of the room. 'Did you actually eat anything?'

'No, but the food looked delicious.'

'You're a very convincing liar.'

'Years of practice.'

They went out to the garden, and Jago spotted his grandfather in his wheelchair, facing the large fountain. Jago gripped Mollie's hand a little tighter and glanced down at her. 'Ready for a showdown?'

Her features were cast in lines of worry. 'I'm not sure any good will come out of cross-examining a fragile, old man.'

'He might be physically frail, but his mind is strong, and I won't allow him to get away with what he's done.'

Mollie didn't answer, but he heard her give a ragged sigh. Jago was not going to stop until he had answers to questions no grandson should ever have to ask a grandfather, but needs must. His and Mollie's future depended on it.

Maxwell must have heard the crunch of their footsteps on the gravel pathway for he turned his chair around to face them as they approached. 'I thought that was Jim to take me inside,' he said with a scowl.

'I want a word with you,' Jago said.

His grandfather straightened in his chair with effort, his hands gripping the armrests with white-knuckled force. 'Isn't it time you took Mollie back where she came from? You have no future with her. She's wrong for you.'

Jago clenched his jaw so tightly he thought he might crack a molar or two. 'I know about the images.'

Maxwell's bushy brows snapped together in a

frown, and he aimed his flashing gaze at Mollie. 'You told him?'

'No,' Mollie said.

'I found them myself,' Jago said. 'On a burner phone in the safe. I've been thinking about it for a while now. Why did the supposed blackmailer contact you and not me? Mollie was my fiancée. I should have been the target of an extortion event, but I wasn't. Why was that?'

Maxwell's gaze lost some of its fire, and he seemed to sink further into his chair. 'What does it matter now? I got rid of the problem.'

'The problem being me?' Mollie said with quiet dignity.

Maxwell disregarded her comment and railed at Jago. 'I couldn't allow you to end up like your father, madly obsessed with a woman who wasn't good enough for him. Their obsession with each other led to their deaths. Do you think I wanted that for you? I had to put a stop to it.'

'You orchestrated those images,' Jago said through clenched teeth. 'There was no blackmailer, was there? It was you the whole time.'

Mollie gasped. '*You* did it? Was I really that bad a choice of bride?'

'It wasn't about you personally,' Maxwell said. 'I needed to disentangle Jago from a relationship that could have led him down the same path as his father.'

'My father loved my mother,' Jago said.

'Love?' Maxwell made a scoffing sound. 'That

wasn't love, it was obsession. They were more interested in themselves than anyone else. Their obsession with each other was more important than their careers, their family, their children. And it led to their deaths, making you and your brothers orphans, ruining my and your grandmother's lives in the process. I saw it happening all over again with you, history repeating itself. I had to stop you. I couldn't stop your father, but I had a moral responsibility to stop you from destroying yourself.'

'I hardly think you're the right person to lecture anyone on moral responsibility,' Jago threw back. 'Who else has those images? You're a smart man, but your computer skills are not up to the task of creating deepfakes as professional as those.'

Maxwell glared back at him. 'I paid someone to do it, but they did it in my presence on that phone so there were no copies. I paid them in cash so there wasn't a paper trail.'

'So why did you keep the images on that phone?' Mollie asked in an anguished tone that clawed at Jago's heart.

'In case you dared to come back,' Maxwell said. 'It was my insurance policy.'

'Mollie didn't breach your damned non-disclosure agreement,' Jago said. 'I tried to get her to talk, but she refused to utter a word. Do you realise what damage you've caused? Two years of hell for both of us. How can you ever justify what you did?'

Maxwell's hands tightened even further on the

armrests of his chair. 'Rail at me all you like, but I did it for you. Now, where's Jim? I want to go inside.'

Jago grasped Mollie's hand. 'I'll send him out for you. But first, I want to make something clear. I don't know who generated those images for you, but they belong in jail. And frankly, so do you.'

Maxwell growled like a grumpy old animal confined to a cage. 'You can delete the images, and no one will be the wiser.'

'I'll delete the images for Mollie's sake, not yours,' Jago said squeezing her hand firmly in his. 'You no longer have any hold over her or me.' He turned and led Mollie back towards the manor, desperate to get away from the evil his grandfather had wrought. He was furious he hadn't worked it out before now. He had let two years pass without searching for the ugly truth. He had blamed Mollie, believing her to be a gold-digger, when in fact his own grandfather had blackmailed her out of Jago's life. How could he forgive himself, much less his meddling grandfather?

When they got back to their room, Mollie was still trembling from Jago's interaction with Maxwell. No one had ever stood up for her before, and to witness Jago doing so sent a wave of love and admiration through her. 'Was it two years of hell for you?' she asked.

Jago scraped a hand through his hair, his expression still brooding with anger. 'He had no right to destroy your life or interfere with mine. I'm so angry right now I can barely speak.'

'Thank you for what you did for me out there.'

He turned to look at her, his anger slipping into a mask of anguish. 'What did I do for you? I believed the worst of you for two damn years. I should have gone looking earlier for answers. I shouldn't have allowed him to hoodwink me into thinking you were after money.'

'It's in the past. Let's hope it stays that way.'

Jago began to pace the floor, his strides agitated, jerky, restless. He stopped and looked at her. 'Let's go back to London. I can't stand to be anywhere near that man right now after what he's done.'

'But what about your grandmother?'

He let out a rough-edged sigh and pushed back his sleeve to glance at his watch. 'She will have gone to bed by now. I'll call her tomorrow. How soon can you pack?'

'Five minutes. I didn't bring much.' Mollie started gathering her things together, part of her relieved she didn't have to stay a minute longer and yet conscious that the weekend pretending to be Jago's fiancée was coming to an end. Would he want to continue their... whatever it was? Relationship? Fling? Something more?

The drive back to London was mostly silent. Every time Mollie glanced at Jago he was frowning, as if his mind was replaying the tense interaction near the fountain. Even his choice of music on the journey seemed to reflect his mood, the brooding Mahler symphony a perfect soundtrack for the dark emotions running under the surface.

They arrived a couple of hours later at Jago's London townhouse in Bloomsbury. As they entered the beautifully appointed house, a host of memories assailed Mollie. She remembered the first time he had brought her here. The first time they had made love. The first time they had cooked a meal together. His proposal and her eagerness in accepting, even though he hadn't told her he loved her. She had hoped he would do so in the weeks leading up to the wedding, but he hadn't. In spite of the evil meddling of Jago's grandfather, sometimes she wondered if Jago would have ever said those three little words that no one had ever said to her before.

Jago shrugged off his light jacket and hung it inside a cloak room near the entrance. 'I'll bring our bags in while you go and freshen up. Do you still know your way around? Not much has changed since you were last here.'

But everything had changed, not in terms of decor or layout, but Mollie had changed. She wasn't the same woman Jago had brought here two years ago. She was stronger now, more resilient and, ironically, more in love with Jago than ever.

Mollie used the downstairs bathroom rather than go upstairs where she knew so many poignant memories would be evoked. But Jago seemed to be taking a long time to bring in their bags, so she wandered around the house, trying not to think of all the times she had been here in the past as his real fiancée, not his fake one. She looked at the ring on her left hand and wondered how anyone could tell it wasn't real. It looked as real as the diamond-and-sapphire earrings and pendant she wore.

On her way upstairs, Mollie looked out one of the windows and saw Jago was speaking on the phone near the car. He was leaning against his car and pinching the bridge of his nose as if the conversation was not a pleasant one. Was he filling Jack in on what had happened? Or Jonas? But she didn't sense he was particularly close to either of his brothers. It occurred to her that Jago was as isolated as she was, having no one to lean on in good times or bad. She sighed and continued up the stairs until she came to his bedroom. She pushed back the door and went in, sweeping her gaze around the room. Not much had changed. The walls were still white, the bed linen of the highest quality, the bedside table lamps crystal and brass. The carpet was deep and plush, and the ensuite as luxurious as ever with a walk-in shower with a rainwater showerhead and twin basins and mirrors along the other wall. There were no feminine items on the second sink, only Jago's shaving kit and cologne on the first. Had anyone shared this space with him in the two years they had been apart? He had said he hadn't dated anyone for the first year. What did that mean? Did it mean he'd still cared for her? Missed her more than he wanted to admit? Or was she being a fool for still hoping he'd loved her when he had never articulated it? There were times both in the past and now where he acted like a man in love. Was it enough to rely on his behaviour instead of a verbal acknowledgement of his feelings? She longed for him to be the first person to say those words to her. Was it foolish of her to hope a second time around that he would?

Mollie left his bedroom and opened the door of the spare room, her eyes widening in shock when she was confronted by a wedding cake—*her* wedding cake—standing on a table out of direct sunlight. The four-tiered cake was still intact, although the frosting looked cracked in places, like old bone china. The marzipan bride and groom embracing on the top of the cake were startling lookalikes of her and Jago, which was an indication of the expertise of the wedding cake designer Tessa Macclesfield. Mollie moved closer to the cake, staring at it like it was a ghost or an apparition, a conjuring of her own imagination. She reached out a hand and touched the delicate lacework icing that bordered the top and bottom of every tier. A tiny piece came away and dropped on the table with a soft plink that made a shiver scuttle down her spine.

Jago had kept the cake.

Mollie couldn't stop looking at the cake, wondering what had motivated him to keep it. Given the circumstances, wouldn't he have got the servants at Wildewood Manor to destroy it? What else had he kept? She hadn't until this moment wondered what had happened to her wedding dress. The wedding was to have taken place in the lush gardens at Wildewood, so when she left in such a hurry, she hadn't had time to take anything but the most basic items with her. Her eyes were drawn to the wall-to-wall built-in cupboards and she moved towards them like a robot, her hand reaching for the crystal knob on the left-hand door. It opened with a soft squeak, and she gasped at her wedding dress and veil hanging there. Her heart was working its way up her throat, pounding, punching, pummelling until she could barely take a breath. She reached out her hand and touched the silk and lace and trailed it through her fingers.

There was a sound behind her, and she swung around with a gasp, putting a hand up to her throat to see Jago standing there with an inscrutable expression.

'You kept the cake and dress?' Her voice came out in a thin thread.

He walked farther into the room to stand near her but without touching. He waved his hand towards the cake and the dress. 'I know it probably confirms my grandfather's opinion of my obsession with you, but I needed these as a reminder never to propose to anyone again.'

Mollie moistened her lips that felt as dry as the cracked fondant on the cake. 'Is that your only reason?'

Jago's eyes were shuttered, but the line of his lips

was thin. 'I was furious when you jilted me. I had never allowed anyone as close as I allowed you, but you left and I let my anger fester for the last two years.'

'*Close?* You held back so much from me,' Mollie said.

'At least I introduced you to my family,' Jago threw back with a frown. 'You didn't even tell me you had a brother, nor did you tell me the truth about your upbringing.'

Mollie shut the cupboard door, blocking the vision of her unworn wedding dress. It seemed to mock her, so too the wedding cake, both of them a reminder of what she had been so close to having, only to have it snatched away at the last moment. 'I told you I loved you, so I think I was much more emotionally available than you. You've only recently told me a little about your childhood, how it was to lose your parents so tragically. It's not healthy to lock that stuff away and never express your grief. Believe me, I know because I've been doing the same.'

Jago wandered over to the wedding cake, poking it with his finger, a deep frown between his hooded eyes. 'I remember everything about that day, even though I was only five years old.' He drew in a ragged breath and turned to look at her. 'My world, my safe and happy life was snatched away when the police arrived to tell my grandparents about the plane crash. I will never forget the sound of my grandmother's wailing. It went on and on and on like a siren. No one could comfort her. Jack and I did what we could, but Jonas was only three. He was too young to understand how everything had changed in the blink of an eye.'

'Oh, Jago, I'm so sorry. It must have been so dreadful, so painful...'

He made a gruff sound that was dismissive of his suffering, but she could see the shadows of pain in his dark blue gaze. Wounded eyes. Eyes that hid a world of agony behind a shield of arrogance and pride. 'My grandfather was never an emotionally available man, and losing his only child, his only son, made him even more avoidant.' He let out a raspy sigh and continued in a tone laced with sadness. 'Looking back, I suspect he sent Jack and me to boarding school within a month or two of our parents' deaths because he didn't want to be reminded of his loss. Jonas, of course, was too young, but he went to yet another boarding school when he was six.'

'That was so cruel. What about your poor grandmother? Surely having her grandchildren around would have helped her work through her grief?'

He gave her a grim look. 'Not according to my grandfather. We were forbidden to talk about our parents in case it upset our grandmother. All the photos of our parents were locked away so they didn't trigger our grandmother's grief.'

'Do you have any photos of your parents?'

'In my study.'

'May I see them?'

He hesitated for a moment, and Mollie wondered

if she had pushed him too far. But then he blinked a couple of times and indicated for her to follow him downstairs.

A short time later, Jago unlocked a drawer of his desk and leaned down to take out a photo album. He placed it on the desk and pushed it towards her, the desk acting as a barrier between them. 'I managed to find these during one of my visits during the school holidays. We didn't often go to Wildewood during term breaks, as our grandfather mostly sent us to various camps and holiday programs to ease the burden of child care on our grandmother.'

Mollie opened the album to the first page where there was a wedding photo of a bride and groom, presumably Jago's parents. The couple looked at each other with such tenderness and love it brought the sting of tears to her eyes. She blinked them away and said, 'They look so in love, so happy.'

'Yes, well, my grandfather would call it *obsession*, but I believe they did genuinely love each other. I never saw them argue, and they were big on affection towards each other, embarrassingly so on occasion.' There was a hint of a wry smile in his voice.

Mollie traced her finger over the photo behind a plastic shield. 'You look like your father. So do your brothers.'

'The Wilde blue eyes, although Jack's are a lighter shade.'

Mollie turned to the next page and saw Jago's mother cuddling a newborn baby, with his proud father beaming down at his wife and child. She had light brown hair that was similar to her own, and it made her wonder if she would ever get the chance to hold a baby of her own—Jago's baby. The possibility had been there two years ago, but this was now, and their engagement was a charade, not the real deal. She turned another page or two until she got to a photo of his parents and Jago as a baby, this time being held by his father; his mother had a scowling Jack sitting on her knee. Mollie studied Jago's tiny features and his head with its sprinkling of black hair, cradled so gently by his father. 'You were a cute baby.'

Jago grunted. 'Apparently, I wasn't a great sleeper, and Jack was as jealous as hell when I came along. I often wonder why they had a third child, given what a handful we were. But they had a nanny, so I guess that helped.'

Mollie turned through some more pages of the family interacting: welcoming their third son, Jonas, then birthday parties, Christmas, holidays in exotic locations, everyone looking happy and blissfully unaware of what the future held. The last photo in the album was of Jago's parents smiling at each other with a vivid sunset behind them.

'That was the last photo taken of them,' Jago said in a sombre tone.

Mollie closed the album and pushed it back across the desk towards him. 'Why don't you get some of these framed and have them around the house?'

Jago's expression tightened as if invisible strings

were tugging at his facial muscles. 'I don't need daily reminders of what I lost.'

'Then, why did you keep the cake and my dress where you can't help but see them all the time?'

A shutter came down over his features. 'I don't use that room. It's mostly locked.'

Mollie couldn't help thinking that was how he dealt with most things he didn't want to face: he locked them away, his emotions, his grief, his pain. But hadn't she done the same? Reinventing a version of herself, one that didn't contain the distressing baggage of her childhood. All those traumatic memories were locked away, never to be examined, pored over, analysed. 'Do you think it's healthy to lock your strongest emotions away?'

Jago put the album back in the drawer, shoved it closed and turned the key with a sharp click. 'I don't know any other way.'

'You could learn.'

'I'd need to be motivated, and I'm not.' There was a stubborn quality to his voice that was reflected in his gaze.

'Why did you ask me to marry you back then?'

Jago came around from behind the desk and stood next to her. 'I thought we were a good fit.'

'In bed?'

His mouth twisted, and a dark gleam shone in his eyes. 'No one came close to you in that regard.' He reached out and touched her cheek with a faint touch that sent a frisson down her spine. Longing ignited in her core, a deep pulsing ache that begged to be assuaged. 'They still don't.' His voice lowered to a deep burr, and his eyes dipped to her mouth.

Mollie drew in a wobbly breath, caught in the spell of his mesmerising gaze. Her need for him overrode her rational brain, and right now she needed to be rational, not led astray by her emotions as she was last time. 'What are you saying? That you want us to continue our pretend engagement?'

A flicker of something passed through his gaze. 'We both want each other. It makes sense to try again. Marry me, Mollie, and we can do it properly this time. No one is standing between us, no one is blackmailing you out of my life. We can be together now.'

Mollie wanted to say *yes*, but what sort of marriage was he offering? 'Are you asking me as some sort of payback to your grandfather? To thwart his plan to break us up for good?'

A frown drove a trench between his eyes. 'I'm asking you because I want you to be my wife.'

'But you haven't told me you love me. Surely that is a prerequisite for marriage?'

'Love is a fleeting emotion no one can really rely on,' Jago said. 'What you can rely on from me is financial security. That's something you craved all your life, isn't it?'

'Yes, but I also want to be loved. I don't want to be used as some sort of revenge plot against someone.'

'My grandfather has nothing to do with my proposal,' he insisted, still frowning. 'You and I make a good team. We understand each other, we have good chemistry, and this is the most practical and sensible option. To start again, to undo the damage of the last two years. I owe that to you, at the very least.'

Mollie's chest was tight with pain instead of joy. He had proposed marriage, but it wasn't the marriage she wanted. It was no different from his previous proposal. She had changed, but he hadn't. His emotions were still locked away like the photo album.

'Has anything ever been real between us?' Mollie asked, her voice cracking over the words. 'It sounds to me like you want a plus one, not a soulmate.'

'What we have is as real as that ring on your finger.'

Mollie looked down at her left hand in shock. She brought her gaze back up to his. 'It's…real?'

'I got a jewellery dealer friend of mine to track it down. He found it in a pawn shop.'

'Why did you make me think it was fake?'

'It seemed like a good idea at the time.'

'Like when you believed me to be a gold-digger, you mean?'

Jago thinned his lips. 'I apologised for that. I know you're not after my money.'

'And yet you just proposed to me using financial security as one of the benefits of marrying you,' Mollie pointed out bitterly.

'It is a huge benefit. I can give anything you want. I can provide for you and your brother. You won't have to do without a thing.'

'Except the one thing I want the most.'

Jago released a jagged sigh of frustration. 'You're asking too much.'

'And you're offering too little.'

His frown deepened, his eyes flinty. 'So you're not accepting my proposal?'

Mollie stepped back from him in case he touched her. His touch could unravel her willpower in a heartbeat. 'I don't want to end up like your grandmother, married for years to a man who doesn't see her for who she is. Who doesn't love her the way she deserves to be loved and honoured and treasured.'

Anger ignited his gaze like the strike of a match. 'Don't compare me to my grandfather. I'm nothing like him.'

'Has he ever told you he loves you?'

'No.'

'Did your parents?'

His throat moved up and down in a tight swallow. 'Yes.' The word seemed to be forced out of him, and a shadow passed through his gaze like a cloud drifting past the moon.

'Did you say it to them?'

Jago swung away from her and went back behind the desk, one of his hands raking through his hair. 'If you're not going to accept my proposal, then at least consider continuing our relationship as it stands. My grandmother is still not well enough to accept the truth.'

Mollie knew this was her chance, her only chance,

of finally being true to herself. True to what she wanted, needed, deserved. Accepting his proposal would desecrate what she believed a marriage should be, one full of mutual love and respect and loyalty. That was the security she longed for, not financial comfort but emotional safety and surety.

'I can't do that, Jago.'

His expression showed no sign of disappointment. It was as if she had told him she couldn't pick up his dry-cleaning or something equally banal. 'It's your decision. I can't force your hand.'

Mollie pulled the engagement ring off her finger and held it out to him. 'You should have told me it was real. I could have lost it as it's a little big for me now.'

He ignored her outstretched hand. 'So you're running away from me a second time?'

Mollie stepped forward and laid the ring on the desk that separated them. She took off the pendant and earrings and put them beside the ring. 'This is nothing like the last time. Back then, I was running scared, terrified those images would hurt not only me but you and my brother. This time, I'm going with my head held high. I don't deserve to live the rest of my life without true love. I spent my childhood like that, and I will not settle for it in my adult life.'

His jaw worked for a moment, and he thrust his hands in his pockets as if he was trying to control the urge to reach for her. 'You're making a mistake, Mollie. I've never asked anyone else to marry me, only you.'

'So I should be honoured? Grateful?' Mollie said with an incredulous look. 'I lived in abject poverty. I was raised in filth and neglect. I was found with my half-brother beside my dead mother and stepfather three days after they overdosed. I've waited my whole life for someone to say they loved me, and you can't or won't do it, even though you claim to want to spend the rest of your life with me. Well, I'm not grateful or honoured to be your choice of bride. The job description doesn't reflect who I am now.' She turned for the door but only got three steps when his voice stopped her.

'Where will you go?'

She turned back to face him. 'I have enough money left over to find myself a place to live. I don't need or want your help.'

All I want is your love.

'At least let me find you somewhere for tonight so you can think things over,' Jago said.

'I'm a fully grown adult, Jago. I can book myself a hotel room.'

His eyes moved between each of hers as if searching for something. 'You're really saying *no*, aren't you?' His tone contained a note of disbelief as if he had never factored in her refusing him. The notorious Wilde arrogance on display once more.

'I'm really saying *no*.' And then she walked out of the study without a backward glance, although her heart cracked like the fondant on her abandoned wedding cake.

CHAPTER TWELVE

JAGO CONSIDERED RUNNING after her, begging her to change her mind, but he didn't want to acknowledge how much her rejection hurt him. He ignored the pain that seized his chest; he disregarded the ache in his belly, the bitterness and disappointment he could even taste in his mouth. He had unfinished business with Mollie, but she was done with him. He was not the type of man to beg, to weep and wail and gnash his teeth over what he couldn't have. Mollie had made her decision, and he had to accept it, but hot damn, it hurt him in ways he hadn't been expecting. He had been looking forward to continuing their relationship, to bringing it full circle to make up for the lost two years. Those two miserable years that he could not get back. Of course, most of his anger should be directed at his grandfather for thinking he was obsessed with Mollie. Maybe he was for all he could think about was her. The taste of her, the feel of her against his body, the way she smiled at him, the way she melted when he looked at her. But that was to be no longer because she wanted more than he had to offer.

Jago stared at the wedding cake, stale now and falling apart bit by bit. Why had he kept it and the dress? What did he hope to achieve by keeping such souvenirs of a doomed relationship? Doomed not just because of his grandfather's meddling but because Mollie had kept so much from him, the stark details of her childhood, the poverty and neglect no child should suffer from. His own childhood had been marked by tragedy, but at least he and his brothers had had the love of their grandmother. But neither he nor Mollie had opened up about their painful childhoods; they had been engaged to each other but offered versions of themselves, not their true selves. Their public personas, their identities, not the essence of who they really were.

Jago closed the door, telling himself he would get his housekeeper to get rid of the cake once and for all. The wedding dress... His gut tightened at the thought of donating it to charity for someone else to wear. It had been made specially for Mollie. It belonged to her, so he would courier it to her to do with it what she wished. But then he thought of her marrying someone else, and his gut soured and cramped as if he had swallowed poison.

Maybe his grandfather was right: he was obsessed with Mollie, and it had to stop, right now.

Mollie had only just arrived back at her flat in Edinburgh when she got a call from the rehab centre to inform her that Eliot had signed himself out. Despair hit her like a punch, knocking away her hopes and dreams for a full recovery for him. Would this nightmare ever end? How much money had she already thrown at getting help for him? How much had she already sacrificed? Never had she felt so alone in the world. Even when she was in the wretched dosshouse with the dead bodies of her mother and stepfather, at least she'd had Eliot with her.

Now she was on her own.

No one knew where Eliot was. Her imagination made her crazy with horrible scenarios of him injecting a contaminated drug in some dark alley in Glasgow, and there was nothing she could do to stop it.

She had failed. Failed to keep him safe as a child and now as an adult.

Even if she had accepted Jago's proposal, no amount of money could stop Eliot destroying himself. It had to be his decision to accept a long-term commitment to help…which in a strange way was exactly what Jago needed to do. To commit to loving someone instead of avoiding opening his heart out of fear of losing that love like he had lost his parents. Mollie understood the reasons behind Jago's locked-away heart, just as she understood the choices Eliot made came from a place of deep hurt and loss, but it was not up to her to fix either of them. It had taken her a long time to realise it, but there were some things you could not control, could not repair, could not restore.

But you could rebuild, and that was what she was

going to concentrate on now. Day by day, she would work at following her dreams, even though her top dream was for Jago to love her, and that was out of her control. She had other dreams that required her focus, and they would be fulfilling in a different way.

Three weeks later, Mollie attended a week-long skin care workshop in London. It was a costly affair, but attending it was a step closer to her achieving her goal of setting up her own specialised clinic. To her surprise, on booking the conference, she received a Cinderella ticket, meaning both the workshop and her hotel accommodation were fully paid for. It was just the boost of luck she needed. Her brother had finally contacted her, informing her he had moved to London and was doing well by checking in to a daily rehab centre where mentors were assigned to each client to help them on their journey to recovery. It gave Mollie another reason to attend so she could catch up with him to assure herself he was doing okay. She had met with him for lunch, and he was surprisingly sober and assured her he was staying clean. He was working with a therapist he had really clicked with and had since made considerable progress in moving forward without the need to anaesthetise himself with drugs or alcohol. Mollie had to take his word for it, but from what she had seen so far, all seemed to be going well with him.

She wished she could say the same for herself. She was lonely, sad, depressed and despairing that no one would ever love her. The only love she wanted was Jago's, but that was asking for a miracle, and she wasn't so foolish to think there would be two granted her in a lifetime. Shouldn't she be grateful for her brother's improvement? Why push her luck and dream that Jago would finally open his heart to her?

After a long day at the workshop held at a plush hotel in the centre of London, Mollie was about to take the lift to her room when she caught sight of an elderly lady being escorted into the foyer by a female companion. Her eyes widened and her heart began to give a staccato thump when she saw it was Elsie Wilde and Harriet the maid who worked for the Wilde family at Wildewood.

Mollie ignored the lift bell ping as the doors opened and turned and walked towards the women, who both smiled as she approached.

'Mollie, how lovely I caught you just in time,' Elsie said. 'Are you free for dinner with me? I just adore this hotel. Did you know it's one of Jago's? He bought it eighteen months ago, and it's only just finished being refurbished. It's gorgeous, isn't it?'

Mollie's stomach dropped like an elevator with snapped cables. 'Jago's?' she gasped.

Elsie beamed. 'He's the silent sponsor behind the workshop. It's not his usual thing, but there you go. The things men will do for love.'

Mollie opened and closed her mouth like a fish thrown out of its bowl. 'I didn't... I mean I would never have come if I'd—' Was he behind the Cinderella ticket? Had her name been tagged on the booking system so she got in for free? She didn't know what to make of it, wasn't game enough to make anything of it. Maybe the guilt he felt about his grandfather's actions precipitated his generous actions. It might not mean anything had changed with his feelings.

'Now, about dinner. I prefer to dine in my room, if that's okay with you? We'll have a lovely catch-up, and the press will leave us alone,' Elsie said. 'Shall we say in half an hour? I like to dine early these days. I go to bed ridiculously early, especially after travelling down from Wildewood.'

'That would be lovely, thank you,' Mollie said.

Harriet gave her the room number with a smile. 'See you soon.'

Jago was staying back at work to go through the fine details of a property deal contract, but the words were blurring in front of his eyes. He had thrown himself into work just as he had two years ago when Mollie jilted him, but like then, nothing could fill the emptiness of his life now. He used to feel a sense of satisfaction when he signed off on a deal. The chase and the catch were once everything to him. Now he was left with a feeling of *Who cares how big the deal is?* Who cared what he achieved? Who cared how much money he had made? He certainly didn't. He didn't care about anything, couldn't think about anything but Mollie. She had filled the hole in his life for the weekend of his grandmother's birthday, but since she had rejected his second proposal, he was left feeling worse than he had when she jilted him. He had harboured such anger towards her for two years, anger that was now directed at his grandfather. But even that was pointless. Maxwell was hardly likely to change, and Jago had to move on with his life. He couldn't stay in this morose state forever. But he had also directed a load of anger at himself. He could have prevented this last two years if he had gone after Mollie, instead of allowing his wounded pride to stop him from pursuing her. He had gone as far as finding out where she was but did nothing to contact her after a few attempts via phone and text. She had blocked him on her phone, and he had taken it to mean she didn't want any further contact with him. He was furious and frustrated with himself for not trying harder. For not seeing what was there if he hadn't been so blinded by arrogance and pride. He was the one to blame for losing Mollie. Yes, his meddling old grandfather was a huge part of it, but Jago should have trusted her, should have trusted his own heart.

There was a firm rap on his office door, and Jack came in carrying a bottle in one hand. Typical, Jago thought. Jack wasn't one to wait to be invited; if he wanted something, he took it. Jago couldn't imagine his brother languishing for a couple of years over a woman who had left him. He would fill her place with another as soon as he could and not have a moment's conscience about it.

'Hey, got a minute for a drink?' Jack said, strolling over to plant the bottle on Jago's desk and then sat on the chair opposite the desk, legs spread wide in his customary confident pose.

'Since when do we have after-hours drinks together?' Jago asked, narrowing his eyes in suspicion.

'Yeah, I know. We're not that sort of brothers, are we?' Jack said it without any note of regret, simply as a statement of fact.

'So what's up?'

'Have you heard anything from Jonas?' Jack asked.

'No. You?'

A frown pulled at Jack's brow, and a flicker of worry moved through his ice-blue gaze. 'I know he's worked on secret commissions before, but it's been months now. Did I tell you the wedding cake designer he was dating called asking me to tell him to call her? She called me several times. I had to fob her off because before he left, he said he wanted to cut all contact with her. She didn't seem the stalker type. And I thought he had a real thing for her.'

'Since when were you an advocate for relationships? I thought you were the biggest cynic about falling in love?'

Jack gave a lopsided smile. 'Yeah, well, I see too many supposedly in-love couples tearing each other apart in a divorce to be a true believer in happily-ever-after, but Jonas dated Tess longer than he dated anyone else.' He rose from the chair in a fluid movement Jago silently envied. He hadn't exercised in weeks and felt lethargic and listless in comparison to his brother's virile and agile movement.

'Where do you keep the glasses?' Jack asked.

'Third cupboard on the left,' Jago said. 'But what are we drinking to? I'm not in the mood to celebrate anything.'

'Yeah, I got that impression.' Jack took two glasses out of the cupboard and put them on the desk then unscrewed the red wine bottle and poured two half glasses, pushing one towards Jago. 'Here. Get that into you.'

Jago looked at the ruby liquid and screwed up his nose. It was undoubtedly top-quality wine, but he had no appetite for it. 'Sorry, Jack. It's wasted on me.'

Jack took a sip of his wine, then put the glass back on the desk. He folded one ankle over his bent knee, his gaze assessing. 'You don't know what you're missing.'

What Jago was missing was being in a relationship with Mollie, but he didn't want to discuss it with his cynical older brother. He deftly changed the subject. 'How's Gran doing?'

Jack swirled the contents of his glass into a tiny whirlpool, then he met Jago's gaze. 'She's made a miraculous recovery. She's up in town having dinner with Mollie as we speak.'

Jago's jaw dropped open. 'What for?'

'Presumably to eat.' Jack lifted his glass to his mouth in an annoyingly casual manner.

'Damn it, Jack. Why's Gran getting involved? Mollie has made it clear we don't have a future together.' He shoved back his chair and stood, sending a hand through his hair in a distracted manner. 'I can do without any more meddling from either of our grandparents.'

'Listen, mate. You stuffed up your relationship with Mollie, not our grandfather. If she had felt more secure with you back then, I'm sure she would have come to you first instead of allowing Maxwell to manipulate her. You asked her to marry you and put a damn expensive ring on her finger, but the only thing she wanted—which is what most of my female clients want, and my male ones, too, for that matter—is for someone to love them and commit to them.'

Jago gave a scornful laugh. 'So you're an expert on relationships now? The playboy celebrity divorce lawyer who has never dated anyone longer than a couple of days?'

Jack gave a negligent shrug. 'I might not want it for myself, but I can see it can work for other people. You act like you're in love—you did two years ago and even more so now. It was a good ploy to get Mollie to come to Gran's birthday, but at the root of it was your desire to be with Mollie again. It was also a good plan to sponsor her conference in your hotel. You want her back in your orbit.'

Jago held on to the back of his ergonomic chair until his knuckles showed white. 'So what if I want to be with her? I'm not with her now because she doesn't want what I'm offering her.'

Jack leaned forward to put his glass back on the table, flicking Jago a glance. 'Have you told her you love her?'

'No.'

'Why not?'

Jago worked his jaw for a moment, his chest feeling like it was in an industrial crusher. He wanted to deny it, to say he didn't love her in a romantic sense, but the words just wouldn't come. He didn't want to lie to himself any more. He did love her. He had always loved her, but admitting it opened up the possibility of losing her. But hadn't he already lost her out of his stubborn refusal to own his emotions?

'I can't. It's a thing I can't seem to push past.' He shook his head and let out a whooshing sigh. 'I said it to Mum and Dad when they left for that weekend away, and look how that turned out.'

Jack rubbed at his jaw, the raspy sound of his stubble against his palm overly loud in the echoing silence. 'At least you said it to them. I never did, and I've regretted it ever since.' There was a heaviness to his tone that Jago had never heard in his brother's voice before. Jack the joker. Jack the quick-witted sarcastic one. Jack the cynical and jaded celebrity divorce lawyer who helped hundreds of clients end their relationships. Jack being gravely serious was something Jago had rarely, if ever, seen.

A light bulb went off in Jago's head, shining a light on his mistaken beliefs about himself, about love, about allowing himself to be vulnerable. What would have been worse? Saying *I love you* and never seeing the loved one again, or not saying it and never seeing them again? At least he had told his parents he loved them. Surely Jack had a much tougher regret to weigh him down. 'I'm sorry, Jack. That must be hard to live with.'

Another shrug. 'Life sucks sometimes, hey?' Jack picked up his glass again and took another sip. He lowered the glass from his mouth and looked at Jago. 'As far as I'm concerned, Jonas is the one who missed out the most. He can barely remember Mum and Dad. At least we had a few years with them.'

'Yeah... I guess...' Jago unlocked his hands from the back of his chair.

'So what's the plan? Should I dust off my best man's suit?' A crooked smile lifted the edges of Jack's mouth.

'You mean you still have it?'

'It's a bespoke design. It cost me a freaking fortune. Of course I still have it.'

Jago smiled, a weight coming off his shoulders that made him feel light-headed and excited in a way he had never felt before. 'You'd better bring champagne the next time we catch up.'

'Will do.'

'Now, how about we have some champagne?' Elsie said as she and Mollie sat in front of a sumptuous feast that had just been delivered to Elsie's room.

Mollie gave the old lady a concerned look. 'Should you be drinking alcohol with your memory problems?'

Elsie's eyes twinkled. 'There's nothing wrong with my memory. Not since the before party.'

Mollie stared at her wide-eyed. 'Before the party? But I thought—'

'It's true I lost part of my memory for a short time, but I regained it without telling anyone. Jago, bless him, wanted to be with you, and my fall and my concussion gave him the perfect excuse to convince you to come to Wildewood with him. I was so convinced it would give you both time to fall in love all over again, but I shouldn't have meddled.' She made a regretful little moue with her mouth and continued. 'I'm sorry it didn't work out for you both. I'm furious with Maxwell for what he did to break you up. You're the first person Jago has ever fallen for, and it's so tragic you're not together. I was hoping my birthday weekend would fix everything, but I have a feeling I've only made things worse.'

Mollie reached for Elsie's hand and gave it a gentle squeeze. 'You didn't do anything wrong. It was sweet of you to try, but Jago isn't in love with me. He has never told me he loved me, not the first time around, nor the second. He just wants a marriage partner without being in love with her. I can't be with him unless I truly believe he loves me. I have craved being loved my whole life.'

'Oh, my dear girl,' Elsie said with tears glimmering in her eyes. 'You sound just like me as a young woman. I settled for financial security with Maxwell and devoted my life to our son James to make up for what I lacked from my husband. But then darling James was taken from me, and I couldn't think of leaving Maxwell, even though I was so miserably unhappy. But raising Jago and Jack and Jonas gave my life a purpose. I know this sounds deluded of me, but Maxwell does love each of us in his way. He was never taught to be open with his feelings. He finds emotions very threatening because his father was exactly the same. He punished Maxwell for showing any sign of weakness, which in those days meant showing any sort of emotion or vulnerability. And he particularly finds deep love terrifying and thinks it's more of an obsession than true love. I've tried to break the cycle, but I'm afraid each of the boys struggle with being emotionally available.'

'I can't settle for that sort of marriage,' Mollie said. 'I love Jago with all my heart, but I don't want to be always looking over my shoulder, wondering when he is going to find someone else. I need full commitment. I need to be loved in return.'

'Of course you do. Everyone does. Jago was hit so hard by losing his parents. Jack was always a tough kid, resilient and strong-willed, and he seemed to cope so much better, although who really knows what mark it's left. Jago was more sensitive and emotional, but of course, after the accident, he shut down completely. Jonas was too young to really remember much, although he must remember it on some level.

Even before James and Alice were killed, Jonas was always a serious little boy. They say trauma changes the architecture of children's brains, and I can well believe it. Those darling boys all changed after losing their parents.'

'I'm so sorry. They were so lucky to have you as their grandmother.'

Elsie gave a wistful smile. 'I'd feel even luckier if you were my granddaughter-in-law. But I've done enough meddling. I can only be there for you in any way you need.'

'Thank you. You're so kind.'

There was a sharp knock at the door.

'Oh, that will be the champagne I ordered earlier.' Elsie's expression looked chagrined. 'Perhaps you'd better answer the door and cancel it. I gave Harriet the night off so you and I could spend time together alone.'

Mollie rose to her feet and went across to open the door to the room service staff. But when she opened the door, she saw Jago standing there holding a bottle of champagne and three glasses on a tray. Mollie stared at him, her mouth falling open in shock, her heart leaping to her throat. 'What are you doing here?' she asked in a tone laced with surprise and a tiny sprinkling of hope.

'I'm joining my two most favourite people in the world for dinner,' Jago said. 'Sorry I'm late. Three weeks late, to be precise.' There was a smile in his eyes, and his mouth was curved in a way that made her heart swell with renewed hope and a flood of joy.

Mollie stepped back to allow him in. 'Is your grandmother in on this visit?'

'No. But I'm happy she's here to witness my proposal.'

'Proposal?' Mollie blinked at him. 'I gave you my answer three weeks ago.'

Jago closed the door with his foot and walked farther into the suite. 'Third time lucky, as they say. Hi, Gran.' He put the tray on a side table and then turned to bend down to kiss his grandmother. 'You don't mind me gatecrashing your dinner with my future bride?'

'Not at all, my darling boy,' Elsie said, eyes shining brighter than the crystal chandeliers in the suite.

Jago turned to Mollie and took both of her hands in his. 'Will you forgive me for taking this long to realise I love you with all my heart and soul?'

Mollie's eyes stung with the threat of tears. Happy, joyous tears. 'You're the first person to ever say that to me.'

'I know, and I'm kicking myself for not saying it two years ago, let alone three weeks back. Will you marry me, my one true love? Please say *yes*. I love, love, love you and want to spend the rest of my life proving it to you.'

Mollie couldn't hold her tears back any longer. She threw herself into his waiting arms, relishing how tightly they came around to hold her close to his thudding heart. The heart that had finally unlocked to let her in. 'I love you too, so much, more than I can ever say.'

Jago tilted up her chin so her gaze met his. 'I can't wait to be married to you. I've missed you so much. I can't believe I've been so blind to my own emotions, but I've always locked them away, so terrified of allowing myself to feel anything for anyone in case they were ripped away from me. But stupidly, I allowed that to happen two years ago. I realise now if I had told you what I felt for you, things might have panned out differently. You would have trusted me and come to me when my grandfather manipulated things to get you to go away. Can you forgive me? I don't deserve it, I know. I can't believe what an arrogant prick I've been, asking you to marry me two years ago and not even mentioning how I felt about you. But I'd locked my heart away so long ago, I could hardly recognise my own feelings. But they're real, my love, so very real. I love you and want you by my side forever.'

Mollie hugged him again, leaning her cheek on his broad chest, finally feeling safe and loved and treasured. She had waited her whole life for this moment, and it was a dream come true that it was Jago who had made her feel so loved and wanted. 'I probably shouldn't have put so much emphasis on you saying the words. Your actions were there all the time, but I didn't think they were enough.'

Jago lifted her chin once more. 'I promise to spend my lifetime showing you how much I love you.' He bent down and pressed a lingering kiss to her mouth, sweeping her away on a cloud of happiness that was unrivalled in her experience of life to date.

'Is anyone going to open this champagne?' Elsie piped up with a smile in her voice.

Jago laughed and released Mollie to do the honours with the champagne. 'Sorry to keep you waiting, Gran, but I had important business to see to.'

'Don't mind me,' Elsie said with a fairy godmother twinkle in her eyes. 'Let's have a quick toast to your and Mollie's future, and then I'll retire to bed and you can go to Mollie's room and finish your so-called business.'

Mollie could feel a blush blooming on her cheeks, but she was thrilled that Elsie was the first to congratulate them. Jago poured three glasses of the bubbling champagne and handed her one, and then one to his grandmother, before holding his against Mollie's and his gran's. 'To love and being loved.'

'To love and being loved,' Mollie and Elsie echoed and sipped from their from flutes.

'There's one other proposal I have for you,' Jago said. 'This hotel is one of my investment properties, and I've just finished refurbishing it. It's only been open a few weeks.'

'Elsie just told me about that a few minutes ago,' Mollie said then gave him a searching look. 'Were you behind the Cinderella ticket?'

Jago's eyes glinted. 'Do I look like Prince Charming to you?'

'Yes,' Mollie laughed. 'You're my Prince Charming.' She was still having trouble believing this was happening, that all her dreams were coming true. She wanted to pinch herself, but she didn't want to let go of Jago. It was so wonderful to be held in his arms and know she was there to stay there forever.

'Are you enjoying the skin care conference?' he asked.

'Very much so. It's one of the best training seminars I've ever been to.'

'Well, the proposal I have, my fourth at last count, is for you to take over the management of the day spa in this hotel. Are you interested?'

Mollie gulped back a sob of undiluted joy. 'Are you serious?'

'Perfectly serious.' Jago bent his head to press another loving kiss to Mollie's mouth, finally easing back to gaze down at her with his dark blue eyes gleaming with happiness. 'As much as I'd love to marry you tomorrow, I think we should wait until Jonas gets back from his top-secret mission. Do you mind waiting another few weeks until we hear from him?'

Mollie smiled up at him, her heart almost bursting with joy. 'I'll try and be patient.'

'That reminds me.' He released her momentarily to take out a ring box from inside his jacket pocket. He prised it open and slipped the sapphire-and-diamond engagement ring on her left ring finger.

'Is it real?' Mollie asked with a cheeky smile.

'As real as my love,' Jago said and bent his head to kiss her once more.

'*Ahem*,' Elsie said after a long moment.

Jago and Mollie pulled apart to smile at her. 'Sorry, Gran. Are we boring you?' Jago asked with a grin.

'Not at all, my darling boy, but I think I need to finish my tipple and then let you two lovebirds have some privacy, don't you?' Elsie's smile was teasing but also full of happiness that shone as brightly as the ring on Mollie's finger.

Mollie slipped out of Jago's hold to press a soft kiss on Elsie's cheek. 'Thank you for your part in bringing us back together. You are my fairy godmother.'

Jago put his arm around Mollie's waist and smiled down at his grandmother. 'You had me completely fooled, but Jack was on to you from the start.'

'Yes, well, Jack is nobody's fool, but I couldn't bear to see you so unhappy, darling,' Elsie said. 'But it all turned out brilliantly in the end.'

Jago wrapped his arms around Mollie once more. 'Yes, it did.' And he lowered his mouth to kiss her once more.

* * * * *

Were you blown away by
Fake Engagement Arrangement*?*
Then make sure you don't miss the next instalment
in
the Wilde Billionaire Brothers trilogy,
coming soon.

And while you wait, check out these other stories from Melanie Milburne!

Cinderella's Invitation to Greece
Nine Months after That Night
Forbidden until Their Snowbound Night
One Night in My Rival's Bed
Illicit Italian Nights

Available now!

HARLEQUIN
Reader Service

Enjoyed your book?

Try the perfect subscription for Romance readers and get more great books like this delivered right to your door.

See why over 10+ million readers have tried Harlequin Reader Service.

Start with a Free Welcome Collection with free books and a gift—valued over $20.

Choose any series in print or ebook.
See website for details and order today:

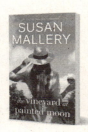   

TryReaderService.com/subscriptions